W9-BSB-868

"I don't need you to take care of me."

"You don't?" Mercury asked. "Was it not my stolen car you were driving?"

"Yes, but—" Sloan stammered.

"Were you not being evicted?"

"Yes, but—"

"Did I not take you to my parents' home for the night?"

"Has anyone ever told you you're rude?"

"Just answer, please."

"Yes, but that doesn't give you the right to think you can control me."

"Look, Sloan. You need help. I want to give it."

"But my father will stop at nothing to get what he wants. He doesn't care who he hurts. I refuse to let you or your family become involved."

"That's not your decision to make. The Steeles can take of ourselves."

"You don't know my father."

"Wrong. Your father doesn't know us."

* * *

Seduced by a Steele by Brenda Jackson
is part of the Forged of Steele series.

Selected praise for *New York Times* and *USA TODAY* bestselling author Brenda Jackson

"Brenda Jackson writes romance that sizzles and characters you fall in love with."
—*New York Times* and *USA TODAY* bestselling author Lori Foster

"Jackson's trademark ability to weave multiple characters and side stories together makes shocking truths all the more exciting."
—*Publishers Weekly*

"There is no getting away from the sex appeal and charm of Jackson's Westmoreland family."
—*RT Book Reviews* on *Feeling the Heat*

"What is it with these Westmoreland men? Each is sexier and more charming than the one before.... Hot, sexy, smart and romantic, this story has it all."
—*RT Book Reviews* on *The Proposal*

"Jackson has a talent for creating the sexiest men and pairing them off against feisty females. This story has everything a hot romance should have."
—*RT Book Reviews* on *Hot Westmoreland Nights*

"Is there anything more irresistible than a man so in love with a woman that he's willing to give her what she believes is her heart's desire? The Westmoreland clan will claim even more fans with this entry."
—*RT Book Reviews* on *What a Westmoreland Wants*

BRENDA JACKSON

———

SEDUCED BY A STEELE

HARLEQUIN
DESIRE

If you purchased this book without a cover you should be aware
that this book is stolen property. It was reported as "unsold and
destroyed" to the publisher, and neither the author nor the
publisher has received any payment for this "stripped book."

Recycling programs
for this product may
not exist in your area.

ISBN-13: 978-1-335-20901-6

Seduced by a Steele

Copyright © 2020 by Brenda Streater Jackson

All rights reserved. No part of this book may be used or reproduced in
any manner whatsoever without written permission except in the case of
brief quotations embodied in critical articles and reviews.

This is a work of fiction. Names, characters, places and incidents
are either the product of the author's imagination or are used fictitiously.
Any resemblance to actual persons, living or dead, businesses,
companies, events or locales is entirely coincidental.

This edition published by arrangement with Harlequin Books S.A.

For questions and comments about the quality of this book,
please contact us at CustomerService@Harlequin.com.

Harlequin Enterprises ULC
22 Adelaide St. West, 40th Floor
Toronto, Ontario M5H 4E3, Canada
www.Harlequin.com

Printed in U.S.A.

Brenda Jackson is a *New York Times* bestselling author of more than one hundred romance titles. Brenda lives in Jacksonville, Florida, and divides her time between family, writing and traveling. Email Brenda at authorbrendajackson@gmail.com or visit her on her website at brendajackson.net.

Books by Brenda Jackson

Harlequin Desire

The Westmoreland Legacy

The Rancher Returns
His Secret Son
An Honorable Seduction
His to Claim
Duty or Desire

Forged of Steele

Seduced by a Steele

Visit her Author Profile page at Harlequin.com, or brendajackson.net, for more titles.

You can also find Brenda Jackson on Facebook, along with other Harlequin Desire authors, at Facebook.com/harlequindesireauthors!

One

Mercury Steele glanced over at his mother, sitting across the breakfast table. Eden Tyson Steele, you just had to love her.

He'd just told her how awful the past few days had been for him. Not only had he lost a client but also one of his prized antique cars had been stolen. She had the audacity to say there must be a reason for the streak of bad luck he'd had lately. Of course, she couldn't resist blaming it on his womanizing ways.

"That's awful about your car getting stolen, Mercury. What did the police say about it?" his father asked with concern.

He appreciated his father's empathy, but then, Drew Steele had passed his love for antique cars on to his six sons. He'd passed something else on to them, as well. Namely his testosterone-driven genes.

In Drew's younger days he'd been quite the ladies' man. His reputation as a philanderer had been so bad that he'd been run out of Charlotte by a bunch of women out for blood—namely Drew's. He had fled from North Carolina, where most of the Steele family lived, and made his way to Phoenix. That was where he'd eventually met and fallen in love with Mercury's mother.

Eden Tyson Steele, a green-eyed beauty and former international model, whose face had graced the covers of such magazines as *Vogue*, *Cosmo* and *Elle*, had practically snatched Drew's heart right out of his chest. Proving miracles could happen.

For the longest time, it seemed their six die-hard bachelor sons had inherited Drew's philandering genes when their womanizing reputation rivaled that of their father's. They'd become known as the Bad News Steeles. Four of Mercury's brothers had now married, leaving only two brothers still single: Mercury and Gannon.

He couldn't speak for Gannon, but Mercury intended to be a bachelor for life.

Their brother Galen was the oldest of the six and had gotten married first. At thirty-eight he'd made millions as a video-game creator. Tyson was thirty-seven, the most recent to marry, and was a gifted surgeon. Eli, at thirty-six, was a prominent attorney in town and had been the second to marry. Jonas, who was thirty-five and the third to marry, owned a marketing business. Mercury was thirty-four and was a well-known sports agent; and Gannon, who had recently turned thirty-three, had become CEO of the family's million-dollar trucking firm when Drew had retired.

"They will be on the lookout for it, Dad, but I was told not to get my hopes up about getting it back. More than likely it will be dismantled for parts. Knowing that hurts more than anything. That particular car was my favorite."

Drew nodded sympathetically and Mercury appreciated his father's understanding of just how upset he still was about it, even if his mother did not. He glanced at his watch. "I need to get going if I intend to make that appointment. A possible new client."

Getting up from the table, he leaned over and placed a kiss on his mother's cheek. "Thanks for breakfast, Mom. You're still my number one girl." He then glanced over at his father. "I'll talk to you later, Dad."

Ten minutes later he was headed toward his office in the Steele Building. A few years ago, his attorney brother, Eli, had purchased a twenty-story high-rise in downtown Phoenix. Eli's wife, Stacey, owned the gift shop on the ground floor. Their brother Jonas's marketing company, Ideas of Steele, was housed on the fifth floor, and Galen leased the entire second and third floors as a downtown campus for his wife's etiquette schools. Mercury and his brother Tyson jointly leased the tenth floor. Although Tyson was the physician in the family, he'd leased the space as a gift to his wife, Hunter, for her architecture company.

Sharing office space with Hunter worked out great. Mercury liked Hunter and for now they shared an administrative assistant, Pauline Martin. The older woman was perfect and had to be the most efficient woman Mercury had ever met. She knew how to handle him, his clients and his appointments.

The moment he merged into traffic on the interstate that would take him downtown, he blinked. Three cars ahead of him was *his* car. *His stolen car.* He would recognize his red 1967 Camaro anywhere. Hell, they hadn't even bothered changing the license plates.

Moving into the other lane, he tried getting as close as he could. Finally, he was two cars behind. When the driver changed lanes, he did likewise. When the car exited off the interstate, he followed, but now he was three cars behind. He pressed the call-assist button on his car's dash. Within seconds a voice came on through the car's speaker. "Yes, Mr. Steele, how can we help you today?"

"Connect me with the Phoenix Police Department."

"Yes, Mr. Steele."

He nodded, appreciating hands-free technology. Moments later the connection was made. "Phoenix Police Department. May I help you?"

"My car, the one that was stolen three nights ago that you guys haven't been able to find, is three cars ahead of me. I'm tailing them as we speak."

"Your name, sir?"

"Mercury Steele."

"What is your location?"

"Currently, I'm in the Norcross District, at the intersection of Adams and Monroe. If the driver makes a stop, then I will, too."

"Sir, you are advised not to tail anyone or take matters into your own hands. Police in the area have been summoned."

Like hell he wouldn't tail the person who'd had the nerve to steal his car, he thought, disconnecting the call.

Mercury saw the driver making a right turn ahead and he quickly put on the brakes when the car ahead of him got caught by a traffic light.

"Damn!" He hoped he didn't lose the thief. It seemed

to take forever for the traffic light to change and then he turned right at the intersection. Glancing around, he saw he was on a busy street, one that led to the Apperson Mall.

Sloan Donahue didn't have time to go back home and change her blouse, and there was no way she could wear one bearing coffee stains to her job interview. That meant she needed to dash into this clothing store and buy a new blouse and then swap it out in the dressing room with the one she was currently wearing.

She was excited. For the very first time she would be interviewing for a job without her parents' help or interference. She'd left Cincinnati, Ohio, a week ago when her parents tried forcing her into an arranged marriage, saying that in their social circles it was their duty to ensure her future and her fortune. She'd refused. Luckily, her parents' predictions that she couldn't make it on her own and would be returning home in less than forty-eight hours didn't happen. She wouldn't go back if they still expected her to marry Harold Cunningham. And she knew they would.

Sloan didn't care one iota that marrying Harold would be a financial marriage made in heaven. It was her life and future they were dealing with. She didn't love Harold any more than he loved her. For the past six months he'd wined and dined her, romanced her like a good suitor was supposed to. For a short while, she'd almost convinced herself maybe he was falling in love with her and that she could possibly fall in love with him.

Then she'd discovered he was having an affair. She'd received the text message he'd intended to send another woman. When she confronted Harold about it, he didn't deny anything. He admitted to being in love with the woman, but said he would do his "duty" and marry Sloan. However, he wanted her to know that, married or not, he intended for the woman he loved to forever be a part of his life. In other words, he would have a mistress if he and Sloan got married.

When she told her parents to call off the wedding and the reason for doing so, they felt Harold marrying her and keeping his piece on the side shouldn't matter. She should consider the boost the marriage would play in her financial future and suck it up. They'd given her an ultimatum to marry Harold or else. She told them she would take the *or else*.

She needed time away from her family, and wanting to get as far away from Cincinnati as she could, Sloan had looked up an old college roommate who invited her to come to Phoenix. But then Priscilla had unexpectedly had to leave the day after Sloan arrived. Priscilla's boyfriend had finally asked her to marry him and had sent her an airline ticket to Spain.

The good thing was that the rent was paid up and Priscilla told Sloan she was welcome to stay in the house for the remainder of the month. That meant getting a job to have funds to cover the rent for next month. For the past few days she'd studied interview videos on the internet and felt she was ready.

As she rushed into the store, she glanced back at her car. *Her car.* It wasn't the Tesla sports car she'd left behind in Cincinnati, but a car that was probably older than she was. But it ran okay, and she'd only paid three hundred for it. It was hers and that was what mattered.

Since her parents had made good on their threat

and placed a hold on the funds in her bank account, she had to watch her money. No telling what else they would do in order to get her to return home. Well, she had news for them. She would rather endure the hardship of not having the finer things in life she was used to than a forced, loveless marriage.

She knew she would be making decisions she'd never had to make before, decisions her parents had always made for her, but it was time for a change. For the first time in her life she felt a sense of freedom she'd never had before, and she truly loved it.

Two

A feeling of relief swept through Mercury when he located his car. Parking in the space beside it, he quickly got out and glanced around the shops in the mall, wondering where the driver had gone.

He was pissed when he pulled his phone out of his jacket to call the police again to give them his exact location. Putting his phone back, he walked around his car and was glad not to see any dents. Other than needing a good wash job, the old girl looked good. Deciding to check the interior, he pulled his car keys out of his pocket to open the door.

"Get away from my car!"

Mercury snatched his head up and was instantly mesmerized by the beauty of the woman's dark brown eyes, shoulder-length curly hair that cascaded around an oval face, high cheekbones, the smooth and creamy texture of her cocoa-colored skin and one pair of the sexiest lips he'd ever seen on a woman.

He immediately flashed her one of his wolfish smiles and was about to go into man-whore mode until what she'd said stopped him. Then he became blinded to all that gorgeous beauty. "*Your* car?"

"Yes, *my* car. Now get away from it before I call the police."

He crossed his arms over his chest. "This is *my* car. It was stolen from me three nights ago."

"You're lying," the woman snapped.

Calling him a liar was a big mistake. The one thing he despised more than anything was for someone to question his integrity. "If you think that, then by all means call the police. However, you don't have to call them since I already have. You're the thief, not me."

"I am not a thief," she said, feeling brave enough to step closer and glare at him.

"Nor am I a liar," he said, glaring back.

Suddenly a police cruiser with flashing blue lights pulled up and two officers quickly got out. One was Sherman Aikens, one of Jonas's old high school friends. "I see you've found your car, Mercury."

Mercury frowned over at him. "No thanks to you guys who should have been looking for it. And my car was never lost, it was stolen, and she's the person who has it."

"It's my car!"

Both officers glanced over at the woman and Mercury glowered. Instead of saying anything, they just stared at her, male appreciation obvious in their gazes. "For crying out loud, aren't you going to ask to see her papers on the vehicle since she claims to be the owner?" he snapped out at the officers.

Sherman broke eye contact with the woman to frown at Mercury. "I was going to get to that." In a voice Mercury felt was way too accommodating, considering the circumstances, Sherman said, "Ma'am, I need to see papers on this vehicle, because it resembles one reported stolen three nights ago."

"It *is* the one that was stolen three nights ago," Mercury snapped while ignoring Sherman's frown. As far as Mercury was concerned, Sherman could become smitten with the woman on someone else's time.

"Stolen! That's not possible, Officer," the woman said, looking alarmed. "Why would anyone want to steal that car? Look at it. It's old."

Mercury glared at her while Sherman and the other officer unsuccessfully tried hiding their grins. "It's a classic, and if it's so old for your taste, why did you buy it like you claim you did?" Mercury asked her.

"Because I needed transportation and it was in my budget," she said, pulling papers from her purse. "I just bought it yesterday." She handed the papers to Sherman.

Mercury thought it took Sherman longer than necessary to switch his gaze from the woman to the papers. He then said in a too-apologetic voice, "Sorry, ma'am, but these papers are fake."

Shock flew to her face. "Fake? But that's not possible. A nice gentleman sold the car to me."

"That 'nice' man conned you into buying a stolen car," Mercury said, ignoring Sherman's narrowed gaze as well as the woman's thunderstruck expression.

Switching her gaze from Mercury to Sherman, she said, "Please tell me that's not true, Officer. I gave him three hundred dollars."

"Three hundred dollars?" Mercury asked, not believing what she'd said.

Lifting her chin, she added, "Yes, I knew the car wasn't worth that much, but the man looked a little down on his luck and needed the money."

Mercury shook his head. "You got that car for a steal, no pun intended. Do you not know the value of that car? It's worth over two hundred *thousand* dollars easily."

She rolled her eyes. "Don't be ridiculous."

Ridiculous? She had bought a stolen car from someone who she thought was a *nice* man, and she thought *he* was being ridiculous? He was about to give her a scathing reply, but Sherman's look warned him not to do so.

"Yes, ma'am, unfortunately that man did run a scam on you," Sherman said. "I hate you lost all that money. I need you to come down to police headquarters and give us a statement, including a description of the man who sold you the car. We will be on the lookout for him."

"Like you guys were on the lookout for my car?" Mercury said under his breath, but when Sherman shot him a disapproving glare, he knew he'd been heard regardless.

Sherman turned to him. "We're going to have to impound the car. You and Miss Donahue need to come down to police headquarters to give statements."

"But I'm on my way to a job interview," the woman said, suddenly looking distressed.

Mercury refused to feel an ounce of sympathy for her since he too would be late for an interview with a potential new client. Now he would have to reschedule. Every sports agent alive would want to sign on Norris Eastwood, but the parents of the high school senior with plans to go straight into the NBA had sought out Mercury. He hoped being a no-show this morning wouldn't be a negative against him. If it was, then he had this woman to blame.

"Are you okay with that, Mercury?"

When he heard his name, he glanced up. "Am I okay with what?" He saw the other officer had pulled the woman off to the side to take down some information.

"Giving Miss Donahue a ride to the police station," Sherman said.

"Don't you have room in the police car? That's the normal way you transport criminals, isn't it? For all we know, she could be in cahoots with the person who stole my car."

Sherman rolled his eyes. "You don't believe that any more than I do, Mercury. It's obvious she's an innocent victim who doesn't belong in the back of a patrol car. She's no more a thief than we are. Look at her."

Mercury didn't want to look at her, but he did anyway. He immediately thought the same thing he had when he'd first seen her. She was a very beautiful woman. Her features were just that striking. And then there was that delectable-looking figure in a navy blue pencil skirt and white blouse. Sexy as hell. But still…

"Unlike you, Sherman, I refuse to get taken in by a beautiful face and a nice body. Need I remind you, the woman was caught with a stolen car, and I refuse to be that gullible." *Again.* He quickly pushed to the back of his mind the one time he had been and the lasting damage it had caused him.

"Look on the bright side, Mercury. At least you got your car back. You can't blame her for being too trusting."

He could blame her and was in just the rotten mood to do it. "Whatever."

"So, will you give her a ride to police headquarters? The sooner we can get there and plow through all the paperwork, the sooner you can get your car released to you. Then you can forget you've ever seen Sloan Donahue."

"So, where are you from?"

Sloan hadn't wanted to glance over at the man whose name was Mercury Steele, but with his question she felt compelled to do so. She had been satisfied with pretending to view all the sights outside the car's window but now that had to come to an end. It wasn't that she was ignoring him, because to ignore a man who looked like him would be nearly impossible. However, she did have a lot to think about.

Because of her naivete in trusting that man who'd sold her that car, she could have been thrown in jail. She could just imagine her parents' reactions if she'd been forced to call and ask them for bail money. Their accusations that she couldn't fend for herself would have been proved right.

Shifting in her seat, she glanced over to Mercury Steele and asked a question of her own. "How do you know I'm not from here?"

"Trust me. I know."

She raised a brow. "How? My accent?" She honestly didn't think she had one.

"No, it wasn't your accent. It's your looks. I know every beautiful woman in this town. If you were from here, we would have met already."

Was he serious? Sloan studied his profile as he maneuvered the car in traffic and figured that, yes, he was serious. "I'm from Cincinnati, Ohio."

"I represented a kid from there once."

"You're an attorney?"

"No, a sports agent."

She nodded. Although she didn't know a lot about that occupation, other than they brokered deals for athletes wanting to play certain sports for a living, she thought he fit the part. First off, he was a sharp dresser. She was convinced the suit he was wearing was the same designer brand her father and Harold often wore. And then there was this car he was driving. A Tesla, like hers. It was obvious he was a successful man. Why hadn't she noticed that before accusing him of trying to steal her car? A car it seemed was rightfully his.

Sloan released a long sigh and inwardly admitted that, considering the circumstances of how they'd met, she appreciated him giving her a lift to the police station. It was time she told him that and apologized for her earlier accusations.

"Mr. Steele?" They'd come to a traffic light and he glanced over at her. In a way, she wished he hadn't. There was something about his green eyes that unsettled her.

"Yes?"

"I want to apologize for everything. I honestly didn't know the car was stolen."

He didn't say anything and for a minute she wondered if he would. Instead he stared at her. Finally, before turning back to the road, he said, "Apology accepted."

That made her feel better, although to her way of thinking, he'd said it almost grudgingly. "And I want to thank you for giving me a lift to the police station."

"Don't mention it." A few moments later, he asked, "How old are you, Ms. Donahue?"

"Twenty-five."

He didn't say anything, nor did he glance back over at her. Since he'd asked hers, she could ask his. "And how old are you, Mr. Steele?"

They'd come to another traffic light and he did glance over at her when he said, "Thirty-four."

He kept staring at her as if he expected her to say something, and when she didn't, he said, "When you refer to me as Mr. Steele that makes me feel even older. I prefer being called Mercury."

She lifted a brow. "Like the planet?"

He chuckled. "Yes, like the planet, and also like the chemical element. However, I was named after one of my father's favorite football players."

She nodded. "I understand about being named after someone."

He turned back to the road and asked, "Do you?"

"Yes. I was named after my grandfather. I'm Sloan Elizabeth." She missed her grandfather and often wondered how different things would have been had he lived. He'd died of cancer six years ago. She would never forget when her parents had shown up on her college campus to deliver the news to her. At least they'd had the insight to know that receiving such news over the phone would have devastated her.

She snapped out of her reverie and saw they'd arrived at their destination.

"Here we are," Mercury said.

Three

"In case you haven't noticed, Mercury, Sloan Donahue is a beautiful woman."

Mercury glared over at his oldest brother, Galen. The woman's looks were the last thing Mercury was concerned with. He had called Galen because he lived close by, and his wife, Brittany, had dropped him off. Once his car was released to him, Mercury would need someone to drive it to his place.

"If she hadn't bought a stolen car I wouldn't be here."

"True," Galen said. "Instead you could have been at the junkyard looking at what was left after thieves dismantled it, so the way I see it, her buying it was a blessing in disguise for you. Once you get off your indignant high horse, you will realize that, as well."

Galen paused briefly then added, "And another thing. Evidently you've been so into getting your car back that you failed to notice that everything about Sloan screams money. I don't know her story now, but I'd bet in her past she lived a life of wealth. That's obvious from her manicured nails all the way to those designer shoes. And if you took the time to talk to her instead of glaring at her, you would notice her refined voice. She spells high-class any way you want to look at it."

Mercury didn't want to look at it in any way. Galen was too damn observant to suit him. "Whatever," he said, glancing at his watch.

He wondered what was taking so long. He'd given his statement and now Sloan Donahue was behind closed doors giving hers. It had taken him less than ten minutes, but she'd been in there for nearly thirty.

No sooner had he wondered at that than the closed door opened, and she walked out, followed by a smiling detective. Mercury immediately noticed the man wasn't wearing a wedding ring. He would bet the detective had been in that room flirting with Sloan instead of doing his job. Or it could be the other way around. Sloan might have been deliberately flirting with the man for a lighter sentence. Regardless of the circumstances, possession of stolen property was a serious crime.

"Like I said, she's a beautiful woman," Galen leaned over to whisper.

He turned to his brother and frowned. "Need I remind you that you're a married man and the father of twins."

Galen chuckled. "I was making the observation for you, not for me. I am happy being Brittany's husband and father to Ethan and Elyse. In fact, I'm looking out for their best interests. It's about time Brittany got a new sister-in-law and the twins a new aunt, don't you think?"

Mercury's frown deepened. "Go to hell."

Galen laughed but Mercury ignored his brother when the detective and Sloan approached. "Now can I get my car?" he asked the man who was still smiling.

"Yes. I'll complete the release now." The detective then turned to Sloan. "You have my business card. If you need anything, don't hesitate to give me a call."

"I will."

The detective walked off and then Mercury heard Galen ask Sloan, "Are you okay?"

It was then that Mercury noticed the worried expression bunching her forehead. "Well, I do have a slight problem," she said.

Mercury didn't like the sound of that. "What?"

"I don't have a way home."

When she looked at him expectantly, Mercury said, "And?"

"I was wondering if you could drop me off there."

Personally, Mercury was wondering if she'd considered calling Uber, a cab or a friend. He was about to put such a thought into her head when Galen spoke up and said, "Don't consider it a problem. Mercury will be glad to drop you off."

Mercury gave his brother a look that could have turned him to stone, but Galen ignored it and said, "My five brothers and I were raised to treat all females with the utmost respect. If one is ever in need, we are there for the rescue."

Mercury fought to keep a straight face. *Respect? Rescue?* Of the six of them, Galen had been the most notorious womanizer. His reputation had extended from Phoenix all the way to Charlotte, North Carolina, where their Steele cousins lived. Hell, Galen had gotten expelled from school once after the principal found him under the bleachers making out with the man's daughter. And now he wanted to stand here and say he respected women like he'd always done so.

"Our mother wouldn't have it any other way, right, Mercury?"

Mercury rubbed a hand down his face. Galen would have to bring Eden Tyson Steele up at a time like this. "Yes, right, Galen." Mercury would give his brother hell when he saw him alone later.

At that moment the detective came back with Mercury's keys and said to him, "Here you are."

The man then turned to Sloan, smiled broadly and said, "Again, I regret what happened to you and wish you the best in the future."

"Thanks, Detective Fulton."

"And I meant what I said earlier—if you need anything else, just call the precinct and ask for me," the detective added.

Mercury fought not to begin fuming again inside. Why was everyone treating her like the victim when it had been his car that had been stolen?

"You're ready to go now?" he asked Sloan, deciding to break up the little chitchat. It wouldn't surprise him if the detective asked her for a date right then and there. The man could do whatever he liked, but not on Mercury's time.

"Yes. Mercury, I'm ready."

That was the first time she'd referred to him by

name and he didn't appreciate that he liked the way she said it. He then turned to Galen and handed him the key. "Take my baby home and park her in the garage."

"Okay, and there's no reason to rush to your place. Jonas will pick me up from there. He's treating me to lunch."

There was no reason for Mercury to ask why. Those two brothers were always betting against something.

Galen then extended his hand out to Sloan. "It was nice meeting you, Sloan."

"Same here, Galen, and again, you have a beautiful wife and twins."

Mercury lifted a brow. "You know about his wife and kids?"

Sloan smiled. "Yes. He showed me photos."

Galen grinned. "I was keeping her company while you were giving your statement."

"I see." Without saying anything else to Galen, Mercury escorted Sloan out of police headquarters.

Sloan glanced over at the man walking beside her. The man who was too good-looking and she had a feeling he knew it. Otherwise, why would he assume he'd know every single woman he thought beautiful in Phoenix?

But she had a feeling every single woman in Phoenix probably knew him, as well. He was a man a woman couldn't easily forget. Tall with medium brown skin, a strong chiseled jaw and a pair of lips that looked so delicious, it would tempt you to take a lick to test their sweetness. And she couldn't forget those gorgeous green eyes.

When she had used the restroom earlier, two women were talking between stalls after having seen Mercury and Galen. They were familiar with those *green-eyed* Steele brothers. Just from eavesdropping on the women's conversation, she found out that at one time Mercury and his five brothers had been pegged the hottest bachelors in Phoenix. Some even called them the "Bad News" Steeles. Their reputations as die-hard players were legendary. Then real shockers happened when they started getting married, one at a time, leaving only Mercury and his younger brother, Gannon, to fire up women's beds.

She figured there was truth in everything the women had said, especially about the Steele brothers being hot. Although she didn't like Mercury very much and thought his attitude could handle some improvement, his looks were downright gorgeous.

Sloan wished there was a wall somewhere to knock her head against. At this point in her life, being attracted to a man, especially to this one, was ludicrous. She had enough problems on her plate without adding Mercury Steele to the menu.

Walking beside him wasn't easy. His walk was brisk, and she could barely keep up with him, but she refused to let him leave her. He had to be wondering why she hadn't called a taxi or used Uber to get home. He would probably be shocked to know she'd never used either in her entire life. While growing up, her parents had always provided private transportation for her. Then for her sixteenth birthday, they'd purchased her first car and she'd gotten a new one every year since.

It was only after arriving in Phoenix and taking

stock of her predicament that it dawned on her that over the past twenty-five years, her parents had played her right into their hands. They had taken care of her every need, given in to her every whim. She hadn't wanted for anything.

There had been more cash in her bank account than she'd known what to do with and credit cards in her name with unlimited balances. All that had made her completely dependent on them, and shamefully she would admit that for years she hadn't questioned it.

Just because she'd never used other modes of transportation didn't mean she thought she was too good to do so. Today just wasn't a good day to try something new. Especially after what had happened this morning in that dress store.

Her credit card had been declined. A credit card that had been issued through her parents' bank, so she knew who was behind that denial. Her parents were determined to put a squeeze on her so she'd be forced to run back home and be their puppet again. Luckily, after telling the nice saleslady about her job interview, the older woman had helped her get the stain out of her blouse.

With her credit cards canceled and unable to get funds from the ATM, that meant she was low on funds. She'd lost three hundred dollars buying that car and had only less than a hundred in cash on her. When she'd tried calling to reschedule her interview, she was told she would have to reapply. She tried not to feel too sad about that.

Glancing over at the man walking beside her, she noted he was staring straight ahead with a brooding expression on his face. He probably hated being bothered about taking her anywhere again, but she would ignore his mood. After all, if he'd taken better care of his car it would not have gotten stolen and she wouldn't be in this predicament. She knew for her to think that way was absurd, but she didn't care. It was just as illogical for him to think she would have intentionally stolen his car or be in cahoots with the people who had.

"I hope I'm not inconveniencing you again, Mercury."

He glanced over at her and her heart began thumping hard in her chest. The look he gave her wasn't one of annoyance but something else. Something she couldn't quite put a name to. It left her momentarily dazed. Before she could sufficiently recover, the look was gone and replaced by one of indifference.

"No problem," he muttered. "Like Galen said, we were raised to respect women and rescue damsels in distress."

"In that case, you have a very kind mother."

"She is definitely that and I wouldn't trade her for all the tea in China."

Sloan heard fondness in his tone, and she wished she could say the same about her own mother, but she couldn't. It was not that her mother was a bad person because she wasn't. She'd just never made her daughter her priority. Her father hadn't been much better. He never failed to let Sloan know she should have been born a boy, and because she hadn't been, he'd treated her like the disappointment she'd been.

"You're okay?"

She glanced back over at Mercury. They had reached his car. A serious frown marred his forehead. "Yes, I'm fine." He nodded and then opened the car door for her. "Thank you."

She slid onto the car's leather seat and then glanced at him. Their gazes met, and when he stood there a moment, she lifted a brow. "Is something wrong?"

As if her question made him realize he'd been staring, he frowned and shook his head. "No. Nothing is wrong."

He then closed the car door and walked around to the driver's side to get in. He had removed his jacket earlier and she liked the way the dress shirt fit him. It was obvious he worked out. A man didn't get those kinds of tight muscles by doing nothing.

"Your address?"

She blinked. "My address?"

"Yes. If I'm to take you home, then I need to know it, don't you think?"

She swallowed. "Yes, of course." She then rattled it off for him. When he started the car, she asked, "Aren't you going to put it in your GPS?"

He glanced over at her before backing out of the parking space. "No. I'm familiar with the area. How long have you been in Phoenix, Sloan?"

She sighed deeply. "One week tomorrow."

He didn't ask her anything else during the car ride and she was fine with him ignoring her all the way to their destination.

"You're having a yard sale?"

His question made her look at him. "A yard sale? No, of course not. Why would you ask me that?"

"Because of what's going on at your address."

She glanced out the car's window and drew in a sharp breath. Her belongings—the little she'd brought with her—were laid out on a table for everyone to see, and it appeared as if someone was having a sale with her stuff. As soon as Mercury stopped the car, she was out in a flash.

Four

Mercury called out to Sloan, but she ignored him and marched with indignation toward the older woman who was still placing items on the table. Shaking his head, he quickly followed while wondering what the hell was going on.

"How dare you do this!" he heard Sloan yell at the top of her voice, while placing her hands on her hips. "These are my things."

The woman, who looked to be in her late fifties and several inches shorter than Sloan, didn't cower. Instead she placed her hands on her own hips. "I do dare. I am not selling anything, although I should since you're being evicted."

"Evicted? But why?"

"Like you didn't know the check Priscilla used to pay her rent this month wasn't good! It bounced like a rubber ball."

Mercury felt Sloan stiffen beside him and immediately realized she hadn't known what this person named Priscilla had done. "You got a bad check? I didn't know. I'm sure there's a mistake."

"Ha!" the lady said. "No mistake. Take your stuff and go."

"But you can't make me leave with no place to go," Sloan implored. "I'm sure if I call Priscilla, we will have this cleared up."

"Nothing is going to get cleared up. Besides, I already have someone interested in leasing this place and ready to move in. I want you gone."

"Who is this Priscilla and where is she?" Mercury asked Sloan. Personally, he didn't want to get involved, but he didn't like the rude way the woman was talking to Sloan.

She turned to him and he could see the anger in her features. "Priscilla is my roommate from college. She invited me out here but left the day after I arrived. Her boyfriend proposed and sent her a one-way ticket to join him in Spain. Luckily, it was a furnished apartment, and other than dishes and silverware, she packed up her stuff that she didn't want to take with her and put it in storage. She said I could stay here until the end of the month because the rent was paid up."

"Not with a bad check it wasn't," the woman intervened to say. "Now get your things and go."

Sloan turned to the woman. "And I told you that I don't have anywhere to go."

"Not my problem," the woman snapped.

Mercury bit down on his lip. Hadn't he thought the same when told she didn't have a car? However, hearing someone else tell her that didn't sit well with him.

"Thank you for bringing me here, Mercury. I'll be okay."

Did she honestly expect him to leave after hearing her tell the woman that she didn't have any place to go? He shoved his hands into the pockets of his pants. "You will only be okay when you stop trusting people so easily," he said, frowning. First, she'd bought a stolen car from a "nice" man, and now she'd been let down by a friend.

Refusing to let the woman listen to their conversation, he said, "Excuse us." He then took Sloan's hand and led her a few feet away from the older woman's ears. "Listen, I can't leave until I truly know you are okay."

"Thanks for your concern, but I have to figure things out on my own."

He nodded. "And how will you do that and where? Were you telling the truth when you said you didn't have anyplace else to go?"

He watched her nibble on her bottom lip. She then stared into his eyes. "Yes. I was telling the truth. I've been in town just a week and don't know a soul."

He started to say she knew him and Galen. And she also knew Sherman and the overly friendly detective. The detective had even invited her to call him if she ever needed anything. It might be a good time to suggest she take the man up on his offer.

But Mercury knew he couldn't do that. He and his brothers might have notorious reputations, but who was to say Sherman and that detective were better? Besides, Galen was right. Mercury and his brothers might be known for their whorish ways, but thanks to

Eden Steele, they knew how far to take them when it came to a woman in need.

"Do you have the funds to move elsewhere?" he asked. He had a feeling she didn't, no matter what Galen had pointed out about her being high-class. He refused to make any assumptions about her.

"No," she said despondently. "Getting to Phoenix took most of my money. Priscilla had offered me a place to stay until I got a job and was on my feet. I had a job interview this morning at a bank."

He had a feeling it had taken a lot for her to admit all of that. Now he wondered if she would answer his next question. "Are you running away from someone?" *A jealous boyfriend perhaps*, he thought.

She hesitated a minute and then nodded. "Yes."

Since she'd given him that much information, he decided to delve deeper. "Who?"

She paused and then said, "Controlling parents. They were pushing me to marry a man they approved of, Harold. That was fine until he told me marrying me meant he got to keep his girlfriend and that she would be a part of our marriage."

"Excuse me." Mercury was certain he'd heard wrong. He decided to make sure. "You didn't just say the man you were engaged to marry told you he intended to make his girlfriend his mistress, did you?"

"Yes, that's what I said."

Mercury was convinced that now he'd heard everything. "Why didn't you tell your parents?"

"I did."

"And they still wanted you to marry the guy?"

"Yes. I'm their only child and the marriage between me and Harold would help them with a business merger."

Mercury shook his head. It was hard to believe people actually thought that way. Although his mother had been notorious for wanting all six of her sons happily married, but all along the key words were *happily married.* She would not have forced them into anything, not that they would have let her.

"So, I decided to leave Ohio and stay with Priscilla. I found out this morning that my parents put a hold on my bank account and I can't get any cash right now. And they canceled my credit cards."

"They actually did that?" he asked, amazed at how far her parents were taking things.

"Yes. They figure sooner or later, without the financial resources I'm used to, I'll run back home to do whatever they want me to do."

"Which is to marry that prick?"

"Yes."

At that moment, Mercury knew he couldn't leave her here. He had a huge condo, but he couldn't take her there either. His home was sacred, and other than female relatives, he didn't invite women over the Mercury Steele threshold.

"I will give you a chance to go back in the house and grab anything I might have missed bringing out," the woman called, as if she was doing Sloan a favor.

"Go on," he said to Sloan. Although she was trying hard not to show it, he could still detect how upset she was. "You might as well take advantage of her so-called generosity. I will help you get your things repacked."

She slumped her shoulders. "Thanks. And then what?"

"And then we load the stuff into my car and get the hell away from here."

"And go where? I don't know you well enough to go to your place."

"I don't remember inviting you to my place." In a way, he was glad she wasn't suggesting that he do such a thing. "I'm taking you to where you'll be okay for the night."

"Where? To a homeless shelter?"

"No."

"Then where?"

He hesitated briefly before saying, "I'm taking you to my mom."

Sloan tried not to dwell on the fact that this was the third time today that she was being taken somewhere by Mercury Steele, and if he was taking her to his mother's like he said, it wouldn't be the last.

She couldn't believe that she'd broken down and told him everything. The only reason she could think of for doing so was that she needed him to understand that being needy wasn't her choice, but a situation being forced on her.

Now, of all places, he was taking her to his mother's. *His mother.* If Sloan hadn't needed a place to stay for the night, she would have refused. Priscilla's reply to the text she'd sent had said there was no way her check had bounced and that she would contact her bank about it. Priscilla wished she could send her money to tide her over, but she didn't have any extra cash.

Sloan glanced over at Mercury. "Are you sure it's okay with your mom to have an unexpected overnight houseguest?" She figured that would be all the time she needed to come up with a plan B, and she had already sent a text message to Lisa Hall, another friend from college, who was living in Miami.

The car had come to a traffic light and he glanced back at her. "Yes, I'm sure she won't mind."

Sloan raised a brow. "Have you done this sort of thing before? Taken strangers to your mom for the night?"

"No. But I know my mom. She has a heart of gold."

Sloan's mother had a heart of gold, too, but not in the same sense. Both her parents thought money was everything and the only important thing in life was more of it. "Tell me about your mom."

He chuckled. "I'll let you get to know her on your own."

"What about your dad?"

He chuckled again. "Dad loves Mom, and whatever makes her happy makes him happy."

"Your parents love each other?" she asked, surprise flitting across her features.

"Of course. Don't yours?"

"No," she replied without hesitation. "I never thought they did and they confirmed it when I told them about Harold's mistress. They felt a loveless marriage wouldn't be so bad since they'd had one for years."

"They actually told you that?"

"Yes. My parents think wealth, not love, is what makes a good marriage."

He stared at her and then asked, "What do *you* think makes a good marriage?"

She released a deep sigh. "I'm not sure there is such a thing as a good marriage. All I know is that I refuse to be forced into one."

The traffic light went to green and Mercury's attention returned to the road. Just as well, she thought. With parents like his, he wouldn't fully understand parents like hers.

"How did you and this Harold guy meet?"

She glanced over at Mercury, whose eyes were still on the road. "Our families have always known each other. Harold and I began officially dating a year ago." She paused. "He says he loves the other woman, and if he could marry her, he would. However, he's too much of a weakling to stand up to his parents."

What she'd just said was true. She was convinced Harold was so conditioned to do whatever he was told, he couldn't fathom doing anything else. But then, she had been the same way until she'd begun to see that was no longer the way she wanted to live.

"Here we are."

She looked out the windshield as Mercury pulled into the circular driveway of a house that was just as big as the one her parents owned. "Your parents' home is beautiful."

"Thanks."

She felt nervous tension line her stomach.

As if he sensed her anxiety, when Mercury brought the car to a stop, he smiled over at her and said, "Things will be fine. Trust me."

Five

Mercury walked into his parents' home, placed Sloan's luggage down and then glanced around, wondering where his parents were. Both their cars were in the driveway. Suddenly, he heard a sound upstairs in their bedroom and immediately got the picture. He turned to Sloan to find her glancing around. Evidently she hadn't a clue.

Quickly moving to the intercom system on the wall, he pressed the one for his parents' bedroom. "Mom. Dad. I'm here and I have a guest."

Turning to Sloan, he thought the last thing he wanted was for her to figure out what his parents were doing. But then he realized that maybe she should know there were some couples who loved the sanctity of marriage and all the benefits that came with it.

"Come, let me show you my mother's courtyard."

He opened the French doors to the garden that held every type flower imaginable.

"It's so nice out here. Is this the house you grew up in?"

"Yes. My parents knew they wanted a large family and decided to buy a house to accommodate their dream. Galen told you about our brothers, so if you can see the first eight years of my parents' marriage, Mom was pregnant most of the time."

"And loved every moment," his mother said, joining them outside. If she was surprised to find his guest was a woman, she didn't show it.

Not waiting for him to make introductions, Eden Tyson Steele moved toward them, giving Sloan what Mercury thought was a very gracious smile. He'd made the right decision in bringing Sloan here. Extending her hand to Sloan, she said, "Hello, I'm Eden Tyson Steele."

For a minute, Mercury thought Sloan was about to curtsy. He understood. In addition to being an awe-inspiring beauty, his mother's elegant and refined manner had an effect on people. Even now Eden looked as if she'd just stepped off the cover of *Vogue* magazine.

"Mom, I'd like you to meet Sloan Donahue. Sloan, this is my mother," Mercury said.

Eden's smile widened. "Nice to meet you, Sloan. You're a friend of Mercury's?"

"No," he answered quickly before Sloan could. "Sloan and I just met today."

His mother looked up at him. "Oh?"

"It's a long story, and unfortunately, I don't have time to explain since I have an important appointment at the office. She needs you."

Eden lifted a brow. "She does?"

"Yes. I'm leaving her here with you. She'll explain everything."

Then, not waiting for his mother's questions—or Sloan's, for that matter—he quickly headed for the door.

Sloan watched Mercury leave, feeling embarrassed that he was doing so without an explanation to his mother or even a goodbye to her. They might not be seeing each other again. She forced her attention away from the closed French doors and looked at the woman standing in front of her.

Eden Tyson Steele's eyes were the exact shade of green as her son's and she was simply gorgeous. Sloan didn't want to keep staring, but her face looked familiar. The woman still had such a warm smile on her face that Sloan felt even worse.

"I'm sorry," she finally found her voice to say. "I should not have let Mercury bring me here."

"Nonsense. I saw the luggage by the door and wondered who it belonged to. Have you had lunch yet?"

Lunch? She'd barely had breakfast. She had grabbed a doughnut and coffee at the diner on the corner. That was when she'd spilled coffee on her blouse. "No, but I couldn't possibly let you feed me, too. Mercury said I could stay the night, but it's your house and your decision. If you prefer I leave, then—"

"Of course you won't be leaving. I will show you to the guest room, where you can get settled, freshen up and join me and my husband, Drew, for lunch."

"Did I hear my name?"

Sloan turned to see a very handsome older gentleman stroll into the courtyard. Eden's son might have her eyes, but everything else belonged to the man who came over to join them and place an arm around Eden's shoulders. Galen's and Mercury's coloring was a combination of their two parents, but their chiseled, handsome looks were from this man. She couldn't help wondering about the other four brothers. Galen said all six had their mother's eyes, but did they have their father's handsome features?

"Yes, sweetheart." Sloan watched as Eden smiled up at the man with both love and adoration in her eyes. Sloan wasn't sure how she recognized such emotions, since she wasn't around them often, but in this case, she could. "Mercury brought us a houseguest. A friend of his, Sloan Donahue." Then to Sloan, she said, "This is Mercury's father, Drew."

He bestowed a smile that was nearly identical to Galen's. She couldn't say it was similar to Mercury's, since she'd yet to see him smile. "How are you, Sloan?"

She took the hand he extended. "I'm fine, but I need to correct something," she said, looking from Drew to Eden. "I'm not a friend of Mercury's."

Drew lifted his brow. "You're not?"

"No. In fact, I'm almost certain he doesn't like me very much."

"Why do you think that?" Eden asked.

Sloan released a deep breath. "His car was stolen a few nights ago and he found it today…with me driving it." At the surprised look on their faces she said, "I unknowingly bought a stolen car." She then told them about their trip to police headquarters and meeting Galen.

"And Mercury brought you here after leaving police headquarters?" Drew asked curiously.

Sloan shook her head. "No, there's more. It's a rather long story."

Eden smiled and gently patted her shoulder. "And we definitely have time to hear it. Over lunch."

Mercury got off the elevator and walked over to the woman sitting at the huge desk in the reception area. "Good afternoon, Pauline. Have the Eastwoods arrived?"

"Good afternoon, Mr. Steele, and no. They did call and say they were on their way. They got caught up in road-construction traffic."

Good, Mercury thought. The last thing he wanted was to keep them waiting again. "Thanks. I'll be in my office. Please send them in the minute they arrive."

"Yes, sir."

He entered his office and closed the door behind him. After removing his jacket and placing his briefcase aside, he placed his cell phone on his desk before easing down in the chair behind it. He then leaned back to think. Not about the Eastwoods because he felt fairly confident that was a deal in the making.

His thoughts were on Sloan Donahue.

Maybe he should have said goodbye. She would spend the night at his parents' home, which would give her a chance to convince her own parents to unblock her credit cards and bank account. And then she'd be gone.

No matter what she'd told him, he just couldn't fathom anyone's parents holding such a hard-line position when they discovered she'd been evicted. There was no way they would want her living homeless on the streets.

And even if she was right about her parents, once she explained her situation to Eden, his mother would probably make a few calls and secure Sloan a job as a live-in companion to one of the older women at his mother's church. Even if she took the position only temporarily, it would allow her to save money, get her own place and apply for higher-paying jobs.

Either way, Sloan wasn't his concern anymore.

Picking up the paperweight on his desk, he exhaled, thinking about how Sloan had dropped into his day. He would admit that he found her attractive. What man in his right mind wouldn't? However, the woman had issues, and he still couldn't get beyond the fact she'd been driving his car. His stolen car.

His cell phone rang. He clicked it on after checking caller ID. "What do you want, Galen?"

"I thought you would like to know the Camaro is parked safely in your garage. Jonas is here to give me a ride back home, and we figured we should take some of your Scotch, as a thank-you for all our help."

Mercury rolled his eyes. "Kind of early in the day for Scotch, isn't it?"

"Not if we each take a bottle."

Mercury sat straight up in the chair. "You didn't help me that much, and I honestly don't recall Jonas helping at all."

"He came here to pick me up. That's helping. And maybe I should mention that we also washed your car. It was dirty but at least there weren't any dents."

"Yes. Despite everything, I appreciate that. And I guess since the two of you washed the car, that earned you each a bottle."

"Stop being so stingy. It's not as if your booze cellar isn't stocked with enough wine and liquor to last a lifetime," Galen said.

"Whatever."

"So, did you get Sloan home okay?"

A frown touched the corner of Mercury's mouth. "Yes. Just in time to be evicted."

"What!"

"You heard me." He then spent the next ten minutes telling Galen what had happened and the information Sloan had shared with him about her parents.

"I knew it!" Galen said. "I told you she came from money. Please don't tell me you dropped her off anyway and kept going."

"Okay, I won't tell you."

"Mercury!"

"For Pete's sake, stop screaming in my ear, Galen. Of course I couldn't just drop her off, especially after that damn respect-and-rescue crap you told her."

"It's the truth and you know it. So, what did you do? Where did you take her? Please don't tell me to your place."

"You know me better than that. I don't do female sleepovers, houseguests, drop-ins or otherwise."

"So, where is she?"

"At the best place and with the finest people. They know how to deal with issues like hers."

"Ah hell, Mercury. Please don't tell me that in your haste to get rid of her you took her to a homeless shelter."

Mercury rolled his eyes. "No, Galen, I didn't take her to the homeless shelter. I took her to our folks. More specifically, I took her to Mom."

* * *

"So, there you have it," Sloan said to Mercury's parents as she finished off the last of the chicken-salad sandwich Eden had served with chips and a glass of iced tea.

"My parents refused to back down about me marrying Harold. When I left home, I had a small amount of cash and a couple of credit cards in my name. I used most of my cash when I bought Mercury's car."

Sloan drew in a deep breath. Already she could tell that Mercury's parents were different from her own. That made her wonder if perhaps they thought she'd made up the entire thing. "I know what I just told you about my circumstances might be hard to believe, but it's true."

Eden smiled and gently patted Sloan's hand. "Oh, I believe you. In fact, listening to you brought back memories of how Drew and I met."

Sloan was surprised to hear that. "Really?"

"Yes. Like yours, my parents also had money and an arranged marriage in my future. It wasn't that Mark and I didn't get along or that he wasn't a nice guy, but we didn't love each other, and I had other plans for my future. I wanted to be a model and had actually gotten an agent and was doing a few jobs behind my parents' backs right after college."

"What happened?"

"They found out and told me to quit the modeling and instead concentrate on becoming Mark's wife…or else they would stop providing me with anything. Up until then, I'd had the best of everything. Of course, I didn't believe they would do it, try forcing me into a marriage I didn't want. But they were determined."

Eden took a sip of her tea, and the expression on her face let Sloan know she was remembering that time. "I was deeply upset when they threatened to destroy the model agency representing me, and my agent caved in under pressure and dropped me. When I still refused to do what they wanted, my parents took my car and charge cards, as well as closing my bank account, leaving me with very little to my name."

Sloan leaned forward, intrigued by what Eden was sharing and fascinated by how similar it was to her own situation. "What did you do?"

"I was determined to make it on my own, so with only a couple of hundred dollars in my pocket, I did something rather foolish. Something that these days I wouldn't advise anyone to do, especially a woman."

"And what was that?"

"I stowed away in the back of a tractor trailer at a truck stop, hiding behind boxes of auto parts the trucker was hauling from Phoenix to California. At the time I was too upset with my agent and my parents to consider the danger doing something like that involved. Luckily for me, the trucker was this guy here," Eden said, smiling over at her husband. "He said my perfume gave me away and my scent was all over his truck. He'd gone ten miles before he pulled over and found me hiding. He threatened to take me back to the truck stop, but I talked him out of it and persuaded him to take me with him to California. Less than two years later, we were married."

Sloan studied Eden and then recognition dawned. Eden Tyson. This was the Eden Tyson who'd been a renowned supermodel right along with the likes of Christie Brinkley, Cindy Crawford and Naomi Campbell. And she was Mercury's mother? Wow!

"I recognize you now and you're still beautiful," she said in awe, complimenting the older woman.

"Thank you, Sloan."

"And I'm glad your situation had a happy ending."

Eden's smile widened. "And I have a feeling yours will, as well."

An hour later, Sloan walked out of the guest-room bath feeling totally refreshed after her shower. She appreciated Eden and Drew opening their home to her. This was such a lovely guest room. The entire house was beautiful and had the feel of a home and not just a house.

Sloan also appreciated Eden and Drew sharing their story with her. She could see by the way they looked at each other that Mercury had been right. His parents did love each other. That was how it was supposed to be. Although marriage was not in Sloan's plans, if she ever did marry it would be for love and nothing else.

She was about to blow-dry her hair when her cell phone rang. She immediately recognized the caller. Harold. Moving to the bed, she picked up her phone. "Why are you calling me?"

"Thanks to you, the folks, both yours and mine, are mad at me."

Did he honestly call to tell her that? "Not my problem."

"It *is* your problem because now they blame me for you ending our engagement. They've given me one week to have you back here in Cincinnati and planning our wedding. So, where are you?"

If Sloan hadn't known it before, she definitely knew

it now. Harold Cunningham was a jackass, especially if he thought there was a chance for them to get back together. "You don't need to know where I am because there won't be a wedding between us. Ever."

And without saying goodbye, Sloan disconnected the call.

Six

"Is it true?"

Mercury glanced up to find his brothers Eli and Tyson standing in the doorway of his office. Neither believed in knocking, and since Pauline had left early today, they'd taken advantage of not having to be announced.

He really wasn't surprised to see either Eli or Tyson today. Eli's law firm took up the entire twentieth floor and he was known to drop in and talk about his wife and one-year-old son, Elias. Like Galen, Eli had fallen into the role of family man like he'd been bred for the part.

As far as Tyson, the Steele brother who was a gifted heart surgeon, was concerned, Mercury knew, from running into Hunter earlier, that Tyson was here picking her up from work for one of their date nights.

A huge smile touched Mercury's lips. "I guess you guys heard that I signed Norris Eastwood today. It will probably make the news this evening."

"We hadn't heard that," Eli said, coming into Mercury's office with Tyson on his heels.

"Congratulations," they both then said.

"Thanks." Mercury leaned back in the chair behind his desk. "If the two of you didn't know about Eastwood, then what are you asking about being true?"

Eli eased down in one of the guest chairs. "The fact that you took a woman home to Mom. And according to Galen, she's a sizzling-hot looker *and* a prim-and-proper lady. She's just the type a guy *would* take home to his mother. What could you have been thinking? A man never takes a woman home to his mother for any reason unless it's serious."

Mercury rolled his eyes. "Galen has blown things all out of proportion. The woman was down on her luck and needed a place to stay for the night."

"And you honestly think our mother will give her refuge for just one night? If Mom likes her, and Galen is convinced that she will, chances are that woman will stay while Mom turns her into your future bride."

Mercury sat up straight in his chair. "That won't be happening."

"You'll never convince Mom of that," Tyson said. "Have you forgotten how Mom and Dad met?"

"Of course I haven't forgotten. Mom stowed away in the back of Dad's rig."

Tyson was still grinning. "And do you recall just why Mom did that?"

The line of concentration along Mercury's brow deepened. "Yes. She was on the run from her parents…"

His voice trailed off when he remembered. Clearly remembered. He gazed over at his brothers, who were staring at him. Now they were both grinning with a "you really set yourself up for that one" look on their faces.

"I need to talk to Mom," Mercury said, quickly moving to the coatrack and grabbing his jacket. The last thing he wanted was for Eden Tyson Steele to fill her head up with romantic ideas, just because she had ended up marrying her rescuer.

"It might be too late, Mercury. You might as well accept your fate."

He ignored Eli's comment as he briskly walked out of his office.

"And you're sure you'll be okay?" Eden asked Sloan again.

Sloan smiled. Drew and Eden had a prior dinner engagement that they'd offered to cancel. Sloan wouldn't hear of it and refused to disrupt their plans for the evening. "I'll be fine. Since you graciously offered me the use of your computer, I'm going to search the internet for more job opportunities."

"Well, if you're sure, then all right," Eden said, smiling. "You have my phone number if you need me and if you get hungry there's plenty of food in the refrigerator."

"Thanks. I'll be fine."

When Drew and Eden left, Sloan crossed her arms over her chest and thanked her lucky stars. She appreciated Mercury for bringing her here. His parents were super. They'd even suggested she remain with them until she was back on her feet. Of course, she couldn't do that, but she had agreed to stay an additional day. She'd sent a text to her friend Lisa, who'd quickly responded and said she could send her a thousand dollars without any problem. The only problem was on Sloan's end since she had no way of receiving the money with a closed bank account.

Another thing she appreciated was Eden letting her use the computer in her office since the battery in Sloan's laptop had died hours ago. After mentioning to Eden that she spoke several different languages, Eden had asked her if she'd ever considered working as an interpreter. It just so happened that she knew the Miss Universe pageant was looking for someone with her credentials. Eden had a friend with connections to the pageant and would arrange for the woman to talk with Sloan about it.

An hour later, Sloan pushed away from the computer feeling irritated at not being able to open a new bank account online. It seemed that her driver's license number was being blocked for some reason. She sighed, trying not to feel defeated.

She was about to try again with another bank when her phone rang. She hoped it wasn't Harold calling again. Her heart kicked up a beat when she saw the caller was her mother.

She clicked on. "Yes, Mom?"

"We expected you back by now, Sloan Elizabeth. We do have a wedding to plan, sweetheart."

Sloan swallowed deeply, knowing it was going to be one of those conversations. Why had she hoped her mother was calling to tell her that she and her father had been wrong trying to force her into a loveless marriage?

Placing the phone on the desk, she decided to put her mother on speakerphone so she could talk while maneuvering through the sites of several banks. "Sorry to disappoint you. I keep telling you that there won't be a wedding. Why won't you and Dad believe me?" she asked her mother.

"Because we know you. Why are you being difficult? You are only hurting yourself. You know your father. He is going to get his way about this or else…"

Sloan lifted a brow. "Or else what?"

"Or else he's going to make you suffer needlessly. Putting a hold on your funds and credit cards is just the beginning. Do you honestly think it was a coincidence you got evicted?"

Sloan sat up straight in her chair. "Please don't tell me Dad had something to do with Priscilla's check bouncing."

"Okay, I won't tell you."

Sloan rubbed a hand down her face, not believing this, although she knew she should.

She didn't have to wonder how he'd found out about her plans with Priscilla. Her father kept on retainer a man who owned one of the most reputable investigative companies in Ohio. She wouldn't have put it past her father to hack into her phone to retrieve all her text messages and phone conversations with Priscilla. Did he also know about the money Lisa had agreed to send her? Would he try sabotaging that, as well? She then thought about how difficult it was for her to open a bank account online. She suddenly felt uneasy. Perhaps he already had.

"What Dad did to Priscilla's bank account was illegal," she said, not caring if she raised her voice.

"You might think so, but he considers it a necessary means to an end. I don't think you realize just how important your marriage to Harold is for this family."

"And what about my survival, Mom? Better yet, what about my happiness?"

"I've discovered a person can force themselves to be happy under any given situation."

"Happiness shouldn't have to be forced."

"I blame your grandfather for putting all these foolish ideas into your head. Being born a Donahue comes with certain costs that must be paid."

"I refuse to pay them."

"Then you're only asking for trouble, Sloan Elizabeth. Not only for yourself but for any allies you drag into this mess."

A lump formed in Sloan's throat. "What do you mean?"

"What I mean is that your father can be ruthless. Please don't drive him to be that way with not only you, but also with others you might befriend in your quest to disobey us. We know Harold called to make amends. He told us you're being difficult with him, too. It's time for you to stop this foolishness. Harold is coming to Phoenix and we expect you to be nice to him when he gets there."

Like hell she would. Sloan was ready to end the call. She knew that nothing she said to her mother would get through to her, so there was no need to waste her time. "And it's time for you and Dad to stop trying to control me. I won't let you do it. Goodbye, Mom." She clicked off the phone.

"I gather your folks still are causing problems."

Sloan swiveled around in her chair to find Mercury standing in the office doorway.

* * *

"Sorry, I didn't mean to startle you," Mercury said, coming to stand in the room.

Sloan glared at him. "Are you apologizing for eavesdropping, as well?"

He leaned against a file cabinet while remembering how Galen had described her to Eli. A sizzling-hot looker who was also prim and proper. He wholeheartedly agreed with the description and found it fascinating that any woman could be both.

"I didn't have to eavesdrop. You were talking loud enough for the entire house to hear. Where are my parents, by the way?" He wasn't ready to discuss the parts of her phone conversation that he'd heard and wished he hadn't. Doing so would only make him mad about the things her mother had said.

"Your parents went out for the evening. They had a dinner date with another couple."

"Probably the Connors," Mercury said, thinking aloud. Deciding to return to his earlier comment, he said, "Sounds like your parents are trying to stir up trouble for you."

She shifted in the chair, and that was when he noticed she had changed from the skirt and blouse she'd been wearing earlier to a pretty pink sundress. Why did the color pink make her look both sexy and feminine?

"A part of me wishes you hadn't heard that, but in a way, I'm glad you did. Now you can explain to your mother why I left, when she returns." Sloan stood. "I need to go pack."

Mercury shoved his hands into the pockets of his pants. "And just where do you think you're going?"

She shrugged a nice pair of shoulders beneath the

spaghetti straps of her dress. "Not sure, but I have to leave here. I don't know how much of the conversation you heard, but if my father thinks you and your family are befriending me, he will cause problems for you."

Mercury just stared at her. Did she honestly think his family needed to be protected against a man who was acting more like a bully than a father? Mercury had heard what her mother said about Sloan's father's ruthless side. He'd also heard there was a strong possibility her ex-fiancé was coming to town to talk her into going ahead with their wedding plans.

"I don't know where I'm going, Mercury, but I need to leave here."

He shook his head. "Honestly? In the middle of the night, with no place to go and no transportation to get there? And before you even think to ask me to take you anywhere, the answer is no."

He watched her nibble on her bottom lip and wished like hell he didn't feel a tightening in his gut. He didn't like the way his thoughts were going with her. He could accept being attracted to her, since it came with the territory of who and what he was. A reaction to any beautiful woman was automatic. Only problem was that he had no desire to be attracted to this one.

"Okay, I won't leave tonight, but I will be leaving in the morning. That will give me a chance to explain things to your mother."

"Good luck with that." Mercury knew his mother. There was no way Eden would let Sloan go anywhere after she explained things.

"Regardless, I will leave first thing tomorrow for the airport."

He raised a brow. "The airport? To go where and how will you pay for a ticket?"

"I have a college friend living in Florida named Lisa. I contacted her and she said she'll be able to loan me a thousand dollars. I'll use it to hide out somewhere in another state where nobody knows me."

"Another friend you can trust?" he asked sarcastically.

She lifted her chin. "You obviously didn't hear what my mother said about my eviction today."

No, he hadn't heard that part. "What about it?"

"My father was behind that, as well."

An incredulous expression settled on Mercury's face. "You've got to be kidding me."

"Sadly, I'm not." She then told him what her mother had said.

"But how could he remove funds from someone's bank account?" Mercury asked.

"Dad is on the board of a number of national banks. Unfortunately, one of those includes Priscilla's bank. He didn't have the funds removed—instead he probably worked with the banker to have them appear as if they weren't there to accomplish what he needed to have done."

As far as Mercury was concerned, her father was worse than ruthless. He was a tyrant.

"So, as you can see, my father will stop at nothing to get what he wants. He doesn't care who he hurts or maligns in the process. I refuse to let your family become involved."

A frown settled on his face. "That's not your decision to make."

"What do you mean it's not my decision to make?"

"The Steeles can take care of ourselves."

"But you don't know my father."

"Wrong. Your father doesn't know us."

She shook her head. "Look, Mercury, no matter what you say, I *am* leaving town tomorrow."

"Aren't you afraid he will cause this Lisa retribution, as well?"

She shook her head. "No. Lisa's father is a US senator and her mother is a high-profile judge. My father isn't crazy enough to mess with their daughter." Then after she'd thought for a moment, she said, "But what Dad *is* doing is blocking my ability to open a bank account online."

Mercury rubbed his hand down his face in frustration. The main reason he had come here was to meet with his mom and quell any foolish notions she might have about any type of relationship developing between him and Sloan, because it wouldn't be happening. But now, after overhearing that phone conversation, protecting Sloan from her tyrannical father had become more of a priority to him.

"Obviously your father is tracking you with your phone. You need to get rid of it."

She nodded, agreeing. "I'll ditch it. One of the first things I will do when I get the money from Lisa is buy one of those burner phones." Then she asked him, "Do you have a way to receive funds through your phone?"

He had a feeling why she was asking. "Yes."

"Do you have a problem with Lisa sending the money to your bank account since I can't open one of my own?"

"Yes, I have a problem with it."

First of all, he didn't like the thought that she was

willing to be on the run like some hunted animal. And second, he refused to believe her father had a way to block her from opening an account at every damn bank in the country.

"Why?"

He crossed his arms over his chest. Earlier today he would have pegged her as a spoiled, rich woman, used to getting whatever she wanted. He'd even felt she had gotten easy treatment at police headquarters. However, the hurt and humiliation he'd seen during her eviction had been real. He'd even felt her defeat. He was somewhat feeling it now and he didn't like it.

"I prefer not being an accomplice to your cowardice."

An angry look appeared on her face and she was out of her chair in a flash. She got right in his face. "How dare you insinuate that I'm a coward? You don't know me or my parents. You don't know how manipulative they can be to get what they want."

He wished she wasn't standing so close. His gaze suddenly became fixated on the delicious shape of her lips. He was staring at them and not her eyes. Unfortunately, she was too fired up to notice.

Not liking where his thoughts or his libido were headed, in a voice gruffer than he liked, he said, "Maybe it's time you stand up to your parents. Running away is not going to help and they will see that as a weakness to prey on."

"You think I don't know that?" she snapped. "I know my parents a lot better than you, and I'm trying to prevent all of you from getting to know them. Trust me—you wouldn't want to."

She drew in a deep breath, and when she did, the

suction was like a vacuum, drawing his mouth closer...
and she still didn't notice. "Whether you help me or not,
I am leaving Phoenix tomorrow. I'll tell your parents
when they return tonight and that's final."

Mercury wasn't sure what pushed him to make the
next move. It could have been the frustration he felt
at that moment or the proximity of his mouth to hers.
All he knew was that he was trying to talk some sense
into her, and she wanted to give in without a fight. That
annoyed the hell out of him. Reaching out, he pulled
her into his arms.

He hesitated only a moment—long enough for her
to pull away or not—and captured her mouth with his.

He wasn't sure what he expected when his mouth
connected with hers, but it definitely wasn't the way
fire blasted through every part of his body. Nor had
he expected the taste of her tongue to go straight to his
groin. And he absolutely had not expected her mouth
to soften beneath the forceful demand of his.

This was what he would call a mind-blowing kiss,
definitely one for the record books. And the way she
followed his lead with her tongue tugged at everything
male within him.

When the sound of someone clearing their throat
intruded, Sloan all but jumped out of his arms. He released her and turned to find his mother standing in
the office doorway with an unreadable expression on
her face. This wouldn't be the first time his mother had
caught him kissing a girl and he doubted it would be the
last. But he could just imagine what Eden was thinking and he knew he needed to get something straight
before she got any wrong ideas.

Stepping away from Sloan, he said, "It's not what you think. I was trying to talk some sense into her."

Eden lifted a brow. "Oh? Is that how it's done now?"

Mercury released a heavy sigh. "Maybe you will succeed where I've failed. She is about to make a big mistake," he said in a curt tone. Knowing he needed to put as much distance between him and Sloan as he could, he asked, "Where's Dad?"

"In his man cave. Maybe you ought to join him there and chill a minute."

"I think I will." Without giving Sloan a backward glance, he strolled past his mother and out of her office.

Walking quickly, he took the steps down to the basement, where his father's man cave was located. His father stood in front of the huge flat-screen television holding the remote while trying to find a decent channel.

Without bothering to turn around, Drew said, "I saw your car parked in the driveway, Mercury. Do I need to wonder why you're here?"

Mercury slid down on the sofa. "It's not what you think."

Drew turned and looked at his fifth-born son. "It's not?"

"No."

His father stared at him a minute too long to suit Mercury. "Is something wrong, Dad?"

His father shrugged his shoulders. "I hope for your sake there's not."

Seven

Sloan figured she had a lot of explaining to do to Eden. But first she needed to give her head a chance to stop spinning and her body time to cease throbbing.

What man kissed like that? Definitely not Harold and certainly not Carlos Larson, that guy she'd dated in college and the only man she'd slept with.

She hadn't known someone could capture your lips in a way where you felt under siege and too filled with pleasure to do anything but be a willing participant.

"Are you okay, Sloan?"

She glanced at Eden and saw the concern in her eyes. "I guess I need to explain."

"Only if you want to."

She didn't want to, but she knew she should. "I owe you one regardless. You've been nothing but kind. And Mercury was right. He started out trying to talk some sense into me. Then something happened we didn't expect and both now strongly regret. I apologize that you were privy to our foolishness. There is no excuse for our behavior."

"No need to apologize, but why did he feel the need to talk some sense into you?" Eden asked, coming to sit down on the love seat.

"Mainly because I've made decisions about a few things."

"Oh?"

"Yes. I got a call from my mother letting me know my father was behind my eviction today."

"He was?"

"Yes. Mom also informed me that Dad intends to make trouble for anyone who tries to help me out of the predicament they've deliberately put me in."

Sloan noticed that Eden didn't seem bothered by that revelation. Instead she said, "I think you need to start from the beginning."

Sloan told Mercury's mother everything. When she'd finished, Eden didn't say anything for a minute. "All this time I was under the assumption that when they made my father, Elijah Tyson, that they broke the mold. Obviously not, if your father is his clone."

Sloan lifted a brow. "You told me about your father at lunch. Are you saying your father was like mine?"

Eden chuckled. "Close enough. When he discovered Drew had helped me cross state lines, he tried to have him arrested. When that didn't work, he tried destroying Drew's trucking business."

"Oh, my."

"Yes. But Drew was determined not to go any-where, even when Dad tried paying him off. Dad literally disowned me until his first grandchild was born, especially one with the Tysons' trademark green eyes. That's when he began changing." Eden smiled. "You can say Galen captured his grandfather's heart. Then I guess he figured Drew couldn't be all bad since the two of us could make a child so perfect. There was also the fact that Drew had money. He was a self-made billionaire who'd turned his trucking company into a huge success."

Eden paused and then added, "He came around, asking for our forgiveness."

"Did you forgive him?" Sloan asked, coming to sit beside Eden on the love seat.

"Yes, because we knew his apology was sincere. My mother had died and he didn't want to spend the rest of his years a mean and hateful man without any family. By the time my second child was born, I honored my father by giving my son my maiden name of Tyson. All six of my sons were very close to their grandfather until the day he died nearly eight years ago."

Sloan didn't say anything. She had lost her grandfather as well, six years ago. "Do you think I'm making a mistake by running away again?"

Eden reached out and took Sloan's hand in hers. "Only you can answer that. You are an adult and what you decide to do is your rightful decision to make. However, please don't make it on the assumption you have to protect my family, just because we are people decent enough to help a young woman in need."

Sloan took in those words and then said, "I have decisions to make."

Eden nodded. "Yes, but the good thing is that you don't have to make them tonight. Or tomorrow. Our offer still stands. You can stay here for as long as you need."

"Thank you."

Eden stood. "I suggest you get a good night's sleep. I can imagine Mercury was overwhelming. That's how he is when he cares about something—or someone."

Sloan hoped Eden wasn't thinking that way because she'd walked in on Sloan and Mercury kissing. They had just gotten caught up in the moment and the clashing of wills. "He only brought me here because he wants to wash his hands of me."

Eden waved off her words. "Don't worry about Mercury. I'm sure he'll get over it."

Sloan thought that might be true for him, but she had a feeling that kiss they'd shared had affected her in a way she wasn't sure she'd ever get over.

Mercury was trying to show interest in the basketball game on the huge flat-screen. After all, sports was his business and one of the players was someone he represented. However, at that moment, none of that mattered. His thoughts were not on the game, but on Sloan.

What if his mother failed and couldn't talk any sense into her? What if her ex-fiancé found her and tried forcing her back home? Or even worse, what if her father sent a bunch of goons to snatch her back and force her into marriage? And why was Mercury even caring when none of it was his problem?

He blamed his thoughts on that damn kiss. The one that still had his insides tingling from head to toe.

"You okay, Mercury?"

He glanced over at his father, who was looking at

him curiously. "Yes. What makes you think I'm not okay?"

"You're twitching," Drew said evenly.

Yes, he was, but there wasn't a law against it, was there? Of course, he wouldn't be a smart aleck and dare ask his father that. So instead of giving a response, he tried to bring his movements under control. When that didn't work, he was about to stand and start pacing when his mother came down the stairs. He was out of his seat in a flash. "Well, did you talk some sense into her?"

Eden crossed her arms over her chest. "Yes, and I didn't have to resort to kissing her like you."

Drew glanced over at his son and frowned. "You kissed Sloan?"

Mercury drew his hand over his face. "Like I told Mom, I was trying to talk some sense into her. I got frustrated."

"And resorted to taking your frustrations out on her mouth," Drew said, nodding. "I see how that's possible."

"Don't you dare encourage him, Drew," his mother said.

Mercury fought back a chuckle. His father was keeping it honest. Of course Drew Steele would know of such things because he probably helped write the Womanizing 101 playbook.

"So, what did she say, Mom?"

Eden tilted her head to stare at Mercury. "She's staying for now, but if she gets another phone call threatening us, then she just might take flight."

"Her father threatened us?" Drew asked, frowning.

"Yes." Eden then told Drew what had happened.

While she did so, Mercury began pacing. He hadn't liked what his mother said about Sloan possibly changing her mind about leaving. He didn't like that one damn bit.

"So, what's your plan, Mercury?"

He stopped pacing to look at his father. "What makes you think I plan to do anything?"

Drew gave him a level stare. "Chances are Sloan will try to hide from her parents unless you come up with a plan. What have I always taught my sons?"

Mercury didn't have to think twice on that one. When there was a problem, first up was to find a solution. However, this situation was different. Couldn't his father see that? From the way Drew was looking at him, he obviously didn't.

"Fine. I'll come up with a plan."

Eight

Sloan looked at Eden across the breakfast table. "Mercury is helping me take care of some business things?"

"Yes. I expect him in an hour, and he will explain everything." Eden looked at her watch and then smiled at her. "Today I'm spending time with my grandbabies."

Sloan heard the excitement in Eden's voice. In addition to Galen's twins, Eden had a one-year-old grandson from her son Eli and his wife, Stacey. The proud grandmother had shown Sloan a photo of the little boy, and just like her other two grands and her sons, he had green eyes.

"Good morning."

She glanced up to see Mercury walk into the dining room. He moved to where his mother sat and placed a kiss on her cheek before glancing over at Sloan.

She'd wondered how she would react upon seeing

him after that kiss they'd shared last night. The thought had worried her, kept her from sleeping most of the night, until she'd accepted that Mercury Steele had undoubtedly kissed a number of women in his day— for him to do it so well—and kissing her had meant nothing.

She could have sworn she saw something flash in his eyes, but what, she wasn't sure, because just as quickly, it was gone. "Good morning, Sloan."

"Good morning, Mercury."

He then glanced at his watch. "Are you ready?"

She wondered just where he intended to take her. "Where are we going?"

"To the bank to open an account. This bank is owned by my best friend's family. So you don't have to worry about your father getting to the manager. Then I figure you can pick out a car and an apartment."

She was about to remind him she would only have the money Lisa would be loaning her when he said, "There is such a thing as building up your own credit."

Building up my own credit.

She nodded, deciding that made sense. She had to start somewhere, and it would be nice being independent the way she wanted. "Okay."

"My goodness, Mercury. Give Sloan a chance to at least finish breakfast."

"That's okay—I'm fine," she said, pushing her plate aside. The thought of building up her own credit had her excited. "I'll take my plate into the kitchen and be back in a flash."

"No rush."

Well, there was a rush, as far as Sloan was concerned. There was something in the way he was looking at her that had a heated feeling flowing through her. Grabbing her plate, she then headed toward the kitchen. When she got there, she leaned against the counter, needing to take a deep breath. Why did Mercury have to look so darn hot in yet another business suit? And the scent of his aftershave was so masculine it sent spikes of desire through her. And when she looked at him, she remembered how thoroughly he had kissed her and how eagerly she had kissed him back.

The only way she could handle spending any time with him today would be to be on her guard, because whether she wanted to be or not, she was attracted to Mercury.

Mercury watched Sloan leave the dining room and couldn't help but appreciate the gracefulness of her walk. She seemed to glide on air, perfect posture and one hell of a sexy body in a pair of slacks and a blouse.

He was getting frustrated with the way his thoughts were going. He recognized the signs whether he wanted to or not; he desired her.

"Mercury?"

He turned and discovered his mother looking at him with an odd expression on her face. "Yes?"

"I've been trying to get your attention."

He knew that was her way of letting him know she'd noticed the interest he was showing toward Sloan this morning. He didn't like the thought of that. "Was there something you wanted?" Of course there was something she wanted; otherwise, she would not have been trying to get his attention.

Eden smiled. "Thanks for taking time out of your busy schedule to care for Sloan today."

Like he had a choice after what his father had made clear last night. Sloan was his responsibility and he'd needed to come up with a plan to make sure she was taken care of. "No need to thank me. From here on out I will handle her."

The smile was suddenly wiped from his mother's face. "I don't want you to *handle* her, Mercury. I want you to take care of her. I want you to see to her needs and make sure she understands the Steeles are here for her regardless of her father's threats."

Before he could give his mother a response, he heard the sound of Sloan coming back. She had changed out of the outfit she'd had on earlier and into a pretty yellow sundress, one that showed off those appealing shoulders, those gorgeous legs. And her hair was pinned back, highlighting a face that appeared as sexy as the rest of her.

"I'm ready, Mercury."

Her words snapped him out of his intense perusal. Drawing in a deep, troubled breath, he turned to his mother. "Sloan and I will see you later."

Sloan glanced at Mercury as he backed out of his parents' driveway. This was the first time they'd been alone since the kiss they'd shared last night. Should she address it, if for no other reason than to make sure it didn't happen again?

She decided to wait and see if he would mention anything about it, and if he didn't, she wouldn't either. Like she'd told Eden, they'd both acted foolishly and sharing that kiss was something they both regretted. She was sure of it.

Last night before going to bed, she'd looked him up

on the internet. He was a former NFL player turned sports agent who was doing very well for himself. And he was considered one of Phoenix's most eligible bachelors.

"Your best friend's family owns a bank?" she asked when she thought the interior was all too quiet.

He didn't answer until he came to a stop sign on the corner. "Yes. Jaye's family has been in banking for years and they own the Colfax National Bank. Most of the branches are located in Arizona, Texas and Oklahoma. Rest assured—you can open an account without fear of your father interfering."

She nodded. "Thanks, Mercury."

"You're welcome." He paused and then said, "May I ask you something?"

"Yes," she said, glancing over at him, hoping he wasn't about to ask her anything about last night. "What would you like to ask me?"

"While growing up, was there not anyone in your corner? Someone you could depend on? To protect you from your parents' craziness?"

Sloan thought about his questions before answering. "Yes—my paternal grandfather. The one I was named after. He was wonderful. My grandmother died before I was born and he would tell me often that they loved each other very much."

She paused and then added, "Pop always said that he sent my father off to college only for him to become an educated fool by getting mixed up with a woman who'd filled his head with crazy notions."

"What kind of crazy notions?"

"That their marriage was to be a business proposition to grow their wealth. My mother's family had once been wealthy, until they lost most of everything when she was fifteen. She swore she would one day regain that wealth and would never be without money again."

Sloan paused, remembering how her mother would tell her often that money was everything and that you could even buy love. "My father bought into her theory of wealth building, and together, for the past thirty years, they have been doing just that. Building wealth. They had to start somewhere and got a loan from my grandfather. That's when he made them sign a legal document that their first child would be named after him. Otherwise, whatever charity he selected would be entitled to a third of whatever wealth they accumulated."

"Sounds like he didn't take any stuff off them."

"He didn't. He also made them sign an agreement to send me to him at his ranch in Texas every summer. Although they did it, they hated doing so and said he was poisoning my mind with foolishness. As I got older, I saw that Pop was showing me just how wrong they were in trying to control my life."

When he brought the car to a stop at a traffic light, he glanced over at her. "Sounds like he tried preparing you for what your parents were capable of."

She'd thought of that same thing over the years and believed that he was. Not wanting to talk about her family anymore, she asked him something she'd been wondering about. "Yesterday, because of me, you missed an important appointment. Were you able to reschedule it?"

He smiled. "Yes. In fact, I cinched the deal. I signed

on this kid who is great on the basketball court. Now I have to make sure he ends up on the best NBA team."

"Congratulations."

"Thanks. And we've arrived."

She glanced out the window and saw they'd pulled into the parking lot of a huge bank. "Thanks for bringing me here. If you'll give me your cell number, I can text it to Lisa."

He turned off the ignition and glanced over at her. "Why?"

"So she can send the money to your phone."

"That's not necessary." He unbuckled his seat belt and got out of the car to walk around the back and open the door for her. What did he mean it wasn't necessary? She still hadn't unsnapped her seat belt by the time he reached her.

When he leaned over to undo it, she said, "I can do it myself."

He straightened and looked down at her. "I figured you could, but when you hadn't, I began to wonder."

The reason she hadn't was because what he'd said had given her pause. "What do you mean it's not necessary for Lisa to send funds to your phone?"

He leaned against the open door with an annoyed look on his face. "Like I said, that's not necessary."

She frowned. "Then how am I supposed to open a bank account without any money?"

"I'm taking care of it."

She tilted her head to look up at him against the glare of the sun, wishing she'd thought to bring her sunglasses. "You're taking care of what?"

He drew in a deep breath as if he was agitated by her

questions. Sloan didn't care. She wanted an answer. "I asked what you are taking care of, Mercury."

He crossed his arms over his chest and stared down at her. "I'm taking care of everything, Sloan. More specifically, I am taking care of you."

Nine

Mercury wondered if anyone had ever told Sloan how cute she looked when she became angry. How her brows slashed together over her forehead and how the pupils of her eyes became a turbulent dark gray. Then there was the way her chin lifted and her lips formed into a decadent pout. Observing her lips made him remember their taste and how the memory had kept him up most of the night.

"I don't need you to take care of me."

Her words were snapped out in a vicious tone. He drew in a deep breath. He didn't need this. Especially from her and definitely not this morning. He'd forgotten to cancel his date last night with Raquel and she had called first thing this morning letting him know she hadn't appreciated it. It had put him in a bad mood, but, unfortunately, Raquel was the least of his worries.

"You don't?" he asked, trying to maintain a calm voice when more than anything he wanted to snap back. "Was it not my stolen car you were driving?"

"Yes, but—"

"Were you not with me when you discovered you were being evicted?" he quickly asked, determined not to let her get a word in, other than the one he wanted to hear.

"Yes, but—"

"Did I not take you to my parents' home? Did you not spend the night there?"

Her frown deepened. "Has anyone ever told you how rude you are? You're cutting me off deliberately, Mercury."

"Just answer, please."

She didn't say anything and then she lifted her chin a little higher, letting him know just how upset she was when she said, "Yes, but that doesn't give you the right to think you can control me."

Control her? Was that what she thought? Was that what her rotten attitude was about? Well, she could certainly wipe that notion from her mind. He bedded women, not controlled them.

"Let me assure you, Sloan Donahue, controlling you is the last thing I want to do to you." There was no need to tell her that what he wouldn't mind doing was kissing some sense into her again. "I'm merely here to help you."

"If you feel obligated to help, then don't."

He didn't feel obligated; he felt responsible for her. Otherwise, he wouldn't be here. Hell, when was the last time he'd been made to feel responsible for anyone?

Thanks to his dad, he did now. "Look, Sloan. You need help and I'm willing to help you. What does it matter if it's my money or your friend Lisa's?"

She glared at him. "It matters because I know Lisa, but I don't know you."

He rolled his eyes. "Hell, I don't know you either, but I'm willing to help you out. I have been helping you out. Again, I will ask you—where would you have stayed last night had I not made sure you had a decent roof over your head?"

"Why do you keep throwing your help in my face?"

He stared at her, getting more frustrated by the second. "That's not what I'm doing. I'm trying to get you to see, to recognize, that I have been there for you, regardless of how well I know you or you know me."

She began nibbling on her bottom lip, and seeing her do so sent a flare of response throughout his body. It made the muscles beneath his business suit tighten with desire. And if that wasn't bad enough, remembering the taste of those lips and her tongue kicked in his body's most primal reaction with a vengeance.

Glad she was too deep in thought to notice, he moved from where he'd been standing, directly in front of her by the car door, to where his erection wasn't so obvious. "We don't have all day, Sloan."

What he wished he could say was that he could only take so much of his body's intense throbbing.

She glanced over at him. "How much?"

He lifted a brow. "How much what?"

"How much are you willing to loan me?"

He shrugged. "How much do you need?"

"Just enough to tide me over until I get a job." Then

she quickly added, "And earn my first paycheck. Then I will pay you back every penny."

Because he knew she wouldn't accept things any other way, he said, "And I intend for you to do so, but I'm willing to break down the payments into installments so it won't be so hard for you."

She nodded. "Thanks. That will work better."

"Now can we go into the bank?"

He watched her unbuckle her seat belt before easing from the car, not knowing she'd flashed a portion of her thigh in the process. Heat curled inside him, threatening the control he'd thought he'd reclaimed.

Then she stood beside him, dark eyes staring up into his. "Yes, I'm ready."

"No, absolutely not! I will not let you put that much money into my checking account. I'll never be able to pay you back, Mercury," Sloan said, not caring if the man staring at her, the man who owned the bank and who was one of Mercury's closest friends, Jaye Colfax, was doing so with keen interest.

"Mr. Colfax? I'd like a private word with Mercury."

The man stood and smiled. "The two of you can certainly use my office to hash out the details of your bank account."

As far as she was concerned, there was nothing to hash out. There was no way she'd let Mercury deposit twenty thousand dollars into a bank account for her.

"So, what's the problem now, Sloan?" Mercury asked as soon as the door closed behind Jaye Colfax.

She glared at him. "There is no way I can let you open a bank account for me by putting that much

money into my account. It would take forever to pay
you back."

"You don't think you'll eventually get a job?"

"Of course I do."

"And were you not the one who a few minutes ago
made it clear to me, Sloan, that you don't like depending on anyone?"

"Yes."

"Then what's the problem?" he asked, getting to his
feet and then crossing the office floor to where she sat.
She wished he hadn't done that. Every time she saw his
body in motion it did things to her. Things that didn't
make sense. She'd seen Harold move and it had never
made her body hot in certain places. It never tempted
her to glide her hands up his shoulders and abdomen
to see just how tight his muscles were.

"Sloan, I asked what's the problem."

Mercury was now standing in front of her, and when
she looked into his gorgeous green eyes, her pulse actually flickered.

"Did we not discuss this out in the parking lot? Did
you not agree to accept my loan and that you would
pay me back in installments?"

"But that was before I knew how much you would
put into my account. Lisa was only going to loan me
a thousand dollars."

He tilted his head to further stare down at her. "And
just how far do you think you'd get with a thousand dollars? Or do you intend to live with my parents forever?"

"Of course not!"

"Then what's the problem? I'm loaning you enough
money to get started. You'd need to put money down
on a car, put a deposit on an apartment, buy food and

clothes. So, I'm asking for the fifth time, what's the problem?"

Sloan broke eye contact with him, knowing there was no way she could express herself logically while staring into his eyes, even if those eyes were upset with her at the moment. Licking her lips, she stared down at her lap instead, trying to gather her thoughts and not dwell on the heat curling in her midsection.

Drawing in a deep breath, she lifted her head to drag her gaze back to Mercury's face and felt her body warm again under his regard. "The problem is that I don't want to be in your debt, Mercury. I don't want to feel dependent on you."

She heard his frustrated sigh before he said in a calmer voice, "At some point, Sloan, you're going to have to accept that, to get out of this mess your parents have placed you in, you're going to have to depend on someone." He paused a moment and then asked, "Do you prefer that my parents loan you the money?"

"No! I could never accept that from them."

"Yet you were going to accept money from your friend Lisa. I'm offering you twenty times what Lisa was able to loan you. I don't understand why you're putting up such a fight. I've never before known any woman who didn't like spending my money."

His words set her off and she was out of her chair so fast it didn't give him a chance to back up, so he didn't. They were standing so close their bodies were touching, the way they had last night before they kissed. Trying to ignore how his closeness made her feel a little light-headed, she said, "I don't want to become beholden to the one man in town who claims he knows every single woman who lives here."

There, she'd said it. She'd expressed her feelings. Now all she had to do was get a grip on her heartbeat and slow it down. She wasn't sure what reaction she had expected from him, but it wasn't that he'd have no reaction at all. He was still staring down at her, those green eyes holding her captive.

"It shouldn't bother you what woman I know or don't know. I'm being generous. Are you going to let me help you or not?"

A part of Sloan knew she was being too prideful for her own good. She should accept his generous offer with the understanding that she would pay him back. Every cent. No matter how long it took. "Will you put me on a payment plan?"

"I told you that I would. Let me repeat myself. The money is a loan and not a gift."

He hadn't stepped back. Was she imagining sexual vibes that seemed to be pouring off him? And why did it seem as if the air shimmering around them was growing taut? "When?"

He lifted a brow. "When what?"

Was she mistaken or was she seeing desire in his eyes? Would she even recognize it if she saw it? "When can I have it?"

"When do you want it?"

She swallowed. They were still talking about a payment plan, weren't they? "As soon as you can give it to me."

"How about now?"

She nervously licked her lips as naked heat seemed to fill her. And did her hips just move against him? And did he have an erection?

"Now?" she asked, trying to keep up with what he was saying.

"Yes, now."

Then he lowered his head and crushed his mouth to hers.

Ten

The kiss was every bit as raw as it was seductive. That was the way Mercury had wanted it to be. He knew what they'd been discussing and in no way was this what she'd asked for, but at that moment he was un-apologetically getting what he knew they both wanted.

She might not understand the heated yearning passing between them, but he most certainly did. It was there, a deep desire that pulsed and throbbed. A desire he definitely didn't want.

This was how he handled such matters, meeting them head-on. Last night he'd kissed her to drill some sense into her. At least that was what he'd told his mother. What was his excuse this time? What was the reason he'd allowed her to get under his skin enough that he'd been tempted to kiss her again? How did Sloan Dona-hue have the ability to arouse him even without putting forth much effort?

When she wrapped her arms around his neck, he could actually feel anticipation thicken the air. He also felt something else thickening. If he were to ease her a little to the left and then lean forward, he could easily take her on that desk. He was then quickly reminded it was Jaye's desk. His best friend wouldn't like Mercury using his office as a make-out room. That thought reminded him of where they were and what they were doing. It also reminded him that he had to regain control of his willpower and he needed to do it now.

He broke off the kiss and took a step back. The dark heat in Sloan's eyes tempted him to come back, return to her arms and reclaim her mouth. But he didn't. He couldn't. He'd crossed another line today and that wasn't good.

"So," he said, after giving in to temptation and licking his tongue across his lips, as if to make sure her taste still lingered there. "I'm glad I've talked some sense into you, and that you've agreed to the money I'm putting into your account."

He watched her expression. His words had been a reminder of the disagreement they'd been dealing with before the kiss.

"I don't like taking your money, Mercury. I wish there was another way," she said softly, not looking at him.

"There's no other way."

"And I wish you wouldn't kiss me every time we disagree about something and claim to be talking some kind of sense into me."

Was that what she assumed was the only thing driving their kisses? Maybe he needed to enlighten her that there was more to it than that. On the other hand, it might be wiser that he just let her assume whatever she wanted. "Maybe we need to try to be of one accord, then."

"Or maybe you need to keep your mouth to yourself."

He could very well tell her it took two to tangle, and that her mouth had been involved just as much as his. "I'll try." That was the best he could do since he could no longer ignore the attraction he felt for Sloan.

Unfortunately, he was a man used to acting on attractions. Women in Phoenix knew him. They knew he was a die-hard bachelor with no intentions of ever changing. The only thing they got from him were nights of lovemaking with more orgasms than they could count.

"Maybe it's something we need to talk about, Mercury."

He didn't agree. Glancing at his watch, he said, "Let's discuss it later. Right now, we need to take care of opening that bank account and then look for a car and an apartment for you."

Mercury could tell by the mutinous look on her face that she wanted to discuss things now, but there was no way that he could. Namely because he'd done something today that he'd never done, which was to give a woman his hard-earned money. In no way was he a cheapskate when it came to women. Just the opposite. He had no problems lavishing his money on someone if it meant the outcome going the way he wanted.

Expensive dinners, weekends at exclusive and luxurious resorts, beautiful flowers, high-priced purses. You name it and he'd bought it. But never had Mercury Morris Steele dropped twenty grand into a woman's bank account knowing in the end he wouldn't be getting a single thing…except for maybe a few stolen kisses when his patience with her had run its course.

Why kissing her was becoming a habit, he wasn't sure. All he knew was that if her mouth got too close to his, he was driven to taste it. Devour it. Make a damn meal out of it. One he was enjoying way too much. Hell, he was even anticipating it happening again. He honestly liked his way of trying to talk sense into her.

The knock at the door signaled Jaye's return and a part of him was glad. Being in a secluded space with Sloan was putting ideas in his head and that wasn't good. "Come in."

Jaye had the damn nerve to walk into the office smiling. Mercury wished he could knock that silly-looking grin off his best friend's face and could only imagine what Jaye was thinking. "Well, have the two of you reached an agreement?"

Mercury decided to speak up before Sloan did. "Yes, we have. We are opening the account."

Less than an hour later, they'd left the bank and were headed to a car dealership owned by one of his brother Eli's friends, Ronald Taylor. Mercury had called Ronald, who'd promised that one of his car salesmen would be ready to work him up a beauty of a deal.

He glanced over at Sloan. She hadn't said much since leaving the bank. He knew she was still bothered that she would be using his money, but like he'd explained to her, she had to start somewhere and this was it. He'd also had to assure her that his money hadn't come with any strings. He'd almost had to kick Jaye to remove the shocked look on his face when Mercury had made that announcement.

"Do you know what kind of car you want?" he asked now, to break into the quiet of the car's interior.

"It doesn't matter," she said, in a voice that sounded defeated. For the life of him he couldn't understand why she would feel that way. With the money he'd given her she could start the independent life she wanted.

"What kind of car did you have before?" he asked her out of curiosity. She glanced over at him and it seemed a whimsical smile touched her lips. He was so taken by it that the driver behind him had to honk his horn to let him know the traffic light had changed.

"The same kind you're driving now."

He lifted a brow. "A Tesla sports car?"

"Yes. Same year and model, but mine was blue. My favorite color."

He shouldn't be surprised. After all, her parents were loaded and had doted on her to keep her under their thumb. And he shouldn't be surprised that blue was her favorite color. It was his as well, and as far as he was concerned, nothing was prettier than blue. He'd even read once that the color blue had a positive effect on a person's mind and body. He could believe that. That was why he preferred making love to a woman on blue linen.

"No wonder you thought my Camaro wasn't worth much."

He wasn't sure what he expected her response to be, but it hadn't been her throwing her head back and laughing. It was the first time he'd heard her laugh, and the sound did something to him. Emotions within him seemed to come to life. Her laughter was so infectious that he heard himself laughing, as well. How

could he laugh about her thinking that one of his antique cars, his prized possessions, was a POS? It didn't
make sense. Nor did it make sense that he'd opened a
bank account in her name and deposited his money or
that he'd kissed her twice now or that he'd taken time
away from his job to take care of her needs.

"I'm truly sorry about that, Mercury."

"About what?"

"About my reaction to finding out the car I'd purchased was stolen. That just goes to show how much
I don't know about cars. About anything. I'm embarrassed to even say that opening that bank account was
new for me. When I turned sixteen, I was given one for
my birthday and Dad automatically deposited money
into it monthly."

She paused and then added, "I never questioned
how much he was putting into it or why. I never realized my parents were binding me to them in a way they
figured meant I'd never want to break free. It was all
about the money."

Mercury didn't say anything because he knew that
was true for some people. Money meant everything.
The more they had the more they wanted. Although
his mother had been born to wealth, his father had not.
Drew Steele was a self-made man and made sure his
sons followed in his footsteps, and they all had. Nobody had given them anything, which was why Drew
wouldn't agree to let their maternal grandfather set up
trust funds for his boys unless he specified the age of
thirty-two. By that age Drew figured they would have
learned to sink or swim on their own. Luckily, all six
of them had been successful, and the five-billion-dollar
trust fund had been icing on the cake.

"Well, at least you had the sense to break free when you realized what they were doing. Some people wouldn't have minded being dependent on others and not thinking for themselves."

His thoughts shifted to the one-and-only woman he had thought he'd loved. Cherae Blackshear. They had met in college. He'd been in his freshman year and attending college on a football scholarship. Galen, Eli, Tyson and Jonas had warned him about those girls who hooked up with football players they thought were going places. He'd gotten injured in his sophomore year and some thought that would be the end of his football career. Cherae's family, who'd been all gung ho on their relationship, then decided she needed to switch ships since his future no longer looked bright.

Mercury would never forget the day she'd visited him during one of his physical-therapy sessions to break up with him because her parents said she had to. They wanted her to hook up with someone who would be able to take care of her and give her the things they felt she deserved. Namely money.

Cherae cutting him loose like that had messed with his mind and left him not giving a damn about his future or anything else. It had taken his brothers arriving on his college campus ready to beat some sense into him. They'd told him that his biggest mistake had been to fall in love in the first place. Bad News Steeles didn't give their hearts to women. Second, they bashed into his brain that to get even he needed to get his ass back in gear and play football again.

Taking his brothers' advice, he had worked hard, endured all kinds of physical pain during his therapy sessions. But he had gotten back in shape. By his junior year, he was in the college team's starting lineup. In his senior year, sports agents had come out of the woodwork to sign him on with the NFL.

That was when Cherae had tried making a comeback. He'd told her in a not-so-nice way that she would be the last woman he'd ever get serious about again. In fact, thanks to her, he'd happily reinstated his player card and the only thing she could get from him now was laid. He'd run into her a few years ago at one of their college homecomings, and she was still trying to find a rich husband.

"They don't look too busy today," he said, pulling into the lot of the auto dealership.

Sloan glanced around and he smiled at the sparkle he saw in her eyes. "There are so many beautiful cars."

"Yes," he said, bringing his own car to a stop. "And there's one out there with your name on it."

"I'm positive this is the car I want," Sloan said excitedly, smiling brightly at both Mercury and the car salesman. Her smile then faded somewhat when she thought of something. "But can I afford it without any credit history?"

To Sloan's way of thinking, the smile the salesman returned was even brighter than hers. "Don't worry about that, Ms. Donahue. Everything has been taken care of."

She lifted a brow, not liking the sound of that. It reminded her of what salespeople would say when they knew her parents would take care of any debts she incurred. "What do you mean by that?"

Before the man could respond, Mercury said, "What he meant is that he's in the business to make sure the customer gets any vehicle they want, even if it means adjusting the payments to accommodate the buyer. Right, Mr. Lowery?"

The man looked over at Mercury, nodded and then glanced back at her. "Yes, that's right."

"Great! Thanks, Mr. Lowery." Like Sloan had told them, she really liked this car. It was a gorgeous sky blue Chevy Camaro. Same make and model as the red car that had been stolen from Mercury, but this one was the current year and brand spanking new. The exterior was so shiny she could practically see herself, and the interior was a dark blue leather with that new-car smell.

"Now I have my very own Camaro," she said, trying to hold back her emotions. Sloan knew she would love this car forever because it was hers. It was a car she would work hard to pay for and that no one had given to her. It was hers and no one could take it away from her.

"Yes, you have your very own Camaro," Mercury said, smiling down at her.

"How much down?" she then asked the salesman.

He looked at her strangely. "How much down?"

"Yes. How much money do I need to put down on this car?" Sloan figured the more she could put down the lower her payments would be. She only had twenty thousand dollars to work with and there were other things she needed to do with that money, which included putting a deposit on an apartment. She also needed to make sure she had enough to make the first couple of car payments in case she didn't find a job right away.

The man hadn't answered yet, but another question popped in her head. "Are there papers I need to sign?

What about documents showing this car is truly mine? Or do I get them in the end when I pay off the car?" Sloan wasn't sure how that worked since she'd never purchased a car before.

"You will get everything later," Mercury said. "I will make sure all the paperwork is mailed to you."

"But I don't have a permanent address yet," she said, nibbling nervously on her bottom lip. She hoped that wouldn't be a problem getting everything in order in time to make her first payment. Now more than ever it was important that she got a job.

Over breakfast Eden had mentioned her friend Margaret Fowler, the one with connections to the Miss Universe pageant, wanted to speak with Sloan on Monday. Although the pageant was held every December, the job of interpreter was year-round and required a lot of traveling the last four months of the year. The other eight months entailed working from home, communicating with pageant officials who spoke other languages.

"I'll pick it up and deliver it to you."

"Thanks, Mercury." She thought he was being nice about everything. So far, she had only two debts to worry about. The car payment and the money she had to pay back to Mercury for the bank deposit. "When do I get to take my car with me?"

"When you have a place to park it, one you can call your own, since my parents' home has enough cars in their garage already," he said.

She nodded. He was right about waiting to get her own place. "That's fine." She then looked at the salesman. "You will take care of my car until I get it, right?"

The man grinned, probably happy for a sale, Sloan

thought. "Yes, Ms. Donahue. I'll take care of it until you return."

She smiled, feeling good about that. She then turned to Mercury. "How soon can we look for an apartment?" She figured the sooner she had a place of her own, the sooner she could get her car.

"Today is fine, but I suggest we go somewhere for lunch first."

She nodded, thinking that was a good idea. She hadn't eaten since breakfast and it had to be around noon now. "Do you know a place?" she asked him.

"Yes, I know the perfect spot, and it's close by."

Eleven

"This is a nice place," Sloan said, taking a sip of her iced tea and looking around.

"Glad you like it. I come here often for lunch," Mercury replied, trying hard not to stare at Sloan.

Why did she have to look so beautiful?

The waitress came to take their orders and he and Sloan discovered they liked the same kinds of foods. Since she'd never eaten there before, he introduced her to several of his favorite dishes. After they'd placed their orders and gotten refills on their iced teas, he asked her, "What are you looking for in an apartment?"

He liked the way the smile curved her lips when she said, "Definitely something I can afford. Already I'll have two bills to pay. Your loan and a car payment," she said, enthused.

He grinned. "You sound excited."

"I am." Leaning over the table, she said, "Do you know this is the first time I will have bills? Real bills? Bills that I will pay without anyone's help. And I am ready to take ownership of them. It's going to be fun learning to budget my money and knowing how much I can spend. So, to answer your question, all I need is a one-bedroom apartment. Of course, it has to have a bathroom, living room and a kitchen."

"Can you cook?"

She grinned. "No, but I can learn. In fact, I think I'll have fun learning." She took a sip of her tea, then asked him, "Can you cook?"

He took a sip of his own tea and then said, "Yes, I can."

"Who taught you?"

Watching her mouth move dredged up memories of the kiss they'd shared in Jaye's office. Mercury wished he could look at her lips and not remember taking them in a way that even now aroused him. Why did she have to taste so damn good? And why was he recalling her taste?

"I taught myself like you intend to do. I did use cookbooks and, on occasion, some of my mother's recipes. I even took a cooking class once."

"A cooking class? Was it expensive?"

There was no need to tell her that cost hadn't mattered because taking the cooking class had been his and his brother Jonas's way to meet women. Not only had they met single women, but they'd garnered invitations for free home-cooked meals with no-strings-attached sex on the menu. "I didn't think it was and thought it was worth every cent I paid. Maybe you should think about signing up for one."

Shrugging her shoulders, she said, "I will have to see if I can fit the cost into my budget."

She was serious about staying on a budget and he thought that was a smart move. Money wasn't endless. Drew had taught his sons the fundamentals of managing money. It was a lesson none of them had forgotten. Their father hadn't built his trucking business into a multimillion-dollar enterprise by accident. He'd always said, you can't spend money you don't have. Those same words still stuck with the six of them today.

"Your mom might have landed me a job where I'll be doing some traveling at least four months out of the year. I will be talking to the lady on Monday."

His eyebrows lifted in surprise. His mother hadn't mentioned that to him. "Oh, what lady is it?"

"Margaret Fowler."

Mercury nodded. He'd known Ms. Fowler for years. The older woman was a world traveler and he'd always admired her spunk. He'd heard his mother mention that after Ms. Fowler turned seventy-five, she'd liked traveling with a companion since her husband had passed away a couple of years ago. A job as a companion would suit Sloan.

"I assume you'd want a furnished apartment to avoid having a furniture bill," he then said.

"Yes, I do. What about appliances? I don't want to buy any of those either."

He nodded. "Appliances are standard items in most apartments. Even a washer and dryer." He was about to say something else when the waitress appeared at the table with their food.

"Looks good."

It was on the tip of his tongue to tell her that he

thought she looked better. Instead he glanced over at her and said, "You're right—it looks good."

"Are you sure I can afford this place, Mercury?" Sloan asked, glancing around the apartment and loving everything she saw. It was just the right size for her with one bedroom, a nice-size bathroom that included both a tub and walk-in shower, a neat-and-tidy kitchen with a breakfast nook and a living room that extended from a wide foyer. The place was completely furnished.

Then there was the little work-space nook with a desk between the kitchen nook and living room. It would be perfect when she wasn't traveling and worked from home. She wasn't sure she could handle all her good luck in one day when yesterday had been such a disaster.

"Is there anything in here you want to change?" he asked her, glancing around, as well.

"No. I love it. The view of the lake from that window is beautiful. I love being on the fourth floor and the elevator makes it convenient. Paying my first two months of rent in advance was a great idea. Thanks for suggesting it."

Now she didn't have to worry about something unexpected coming up or miscalculating her budget and getting evicted. That was an experience she never wanted to repeat. Glancing at her watch, she saw it was close to three in the afternoon. The apartment manager said she could move in as soon as she wanted.

"I got a lot accomplished today thanks to you, Mercury. Please don't forget to get me that installment schedule so I can start paying you back."

"I won't forget."

"Although I'm sure she probably doesn't need my help with anything, I told your mother I would be back in time to help her with dinner tonight."

"So, you will be there?"

Where else would she be? Was that disappointment she heard in his voice at the prospect that she would be? Eden had explained that every Thursday night was their family gathering for her sons, their wives and the grandkids. Sloan couldn't help wondering if Mercury felt her being there was infringing on the time the Steeles spent together when she wasn't one of them.

"I offered to leave for a while and go to a movie, but your mother wouldn't hear of it." Eden had told her she could use her car whenever she needed to go somewhere since she had a spare. "However, I can certainly change those plans if you prefer I not be there."

He lifted a brow. "What makes you think it matters to me if you are there or not?"

She looked him directly in the eyes. "Your tone just now gave me the impression you'd rather I not be there."

He shoved his hands into the pockets of his pants, making her fully aware of his height and masculinity. "It doesn't matter to me. It's my parents' house and they can invite whomever they want."

Sloan tried not to get frustrated with him and ruin what had been a great day. "I'm very much aware it's your parents' home and they can invite whoever they want, Mercury."

"Then why are you worrying about it?"

She honestly wasn't liking his attitude right now. "I'm not worrying about it. I just didn't want to do anything to make you feel uncomfortable. It's your family and I prefer not intruding if you don't want me there. I'm glad to know you don't care one way or the other."

She moved to walk away and he caught hold of her arm. He didn't say anything when she turned back to him. He simply stood there and held her arm while staring at her. Honestly, there was nothing simple about it. He had a way of looking at her that made something stir inside her.

Her chest had been heaving with frustration; now it was surging with something else. Something she didn't want to feel but couldn't stop herself from feeling. Passion and desire were new to her, but around Mercury she could recognize them for what they were. Only problem was that they had no place in her life now. There were more important things she needed to concentrate on. Learning how to survive without her parents' wealth topped the list. But with Mercury, temptation was hard to resist.

"Is something wrong, Mercury?"

"What makes you think something is wrong?" he asked in a voice that was so husky it seemed to make a crackle of energy flow in the room.

Duh. He was standing there holding her arm while staring her down in a way that made a deep yearning stir to life within her. However, if for whatever reason he refused to acknowledge the obvious, she wouldn't follow his lead. Not this time, even if doing so would be wise.

At that moment she was too mesmerized by the look in his green eyes. The one thing she couldn't ignore was how close he stood to her. The scent of him and the touch of his hand were making her even more aware of him.

Suddenly, he began stroking the tips of his fingers up and down her arm. She nearly closed her eyes on a groan. Fire began running through her veins. And from the heated look in his eyes she had a feeling he knew what he was doing to her and wanted to know—why?

"Why, Mercury?" She figured she didn't have to elaborate. He *had* to know what she was asking.

"I honestly don't know, Sloan. All I know is that whenever I get close to you, I have the urge to touch you. And when we're at odds, all I can think about is kissing you."

His words caused sensations to flow through her. That wasn't good. She was being aroused in a way she'd never been before. "I bet you tell that to all the women."

"Actually, I don't."

Yeah, right. There was no way she could believe him. She understood why women were drawn to him. The man was way too handsome for his own good… and for hers. "What do you want from me, Mercury?" she heard herself ask and then wondered why she'd bothered. It was obvious from the look in his eyes what he wanted.

It wasn't as if she didn't understand the attraction thing; she had just figured it would never affect her. He was proving her wrong. At any other time, she probably would welcome such a diversion as a way to claim her independence, but the timing was all wrong. The man was all wrong. She wasn't certain why she was so sure of the latter, but she was.

"I shouldn't want anything from you, Sloan."

"But you do?"

"I wouldn't be a man if I didn't."

She frankly didn't know what to say to that. He

saved her from saying anything when he pulled her to him and covered her mouth with his, causing bone-melting fire to rush through her. They'd kissed three times now, and each time he did it with toe-curling expertise. When she groaned, he intensified the kiss by slanting his mouth over hers.

Had they finished their discussion? She didn't think so, but this was so much better than talking. Why did his kisses have the power to kick up her pulse, have desire flowing through her? She might not be as experienced a kisser as he was, but Sloan was determined to show Mercury she learned fast and could be just as thorough. His tongue might be swirling all around hers, but she was following his lead. If Mercury's groans were anything to go by, he was obviously enjoying this kiss as much as she was. That made her wonder who was seducing whom…

He surprised her when he let go of her arm only to plunge his hands into her hair as if to pull her mouth closer while his tongue went deeper. His mouth was firm and strong, and his lips were demanding. In the past, all the kisses she'd ever shared with a guy had been controlled, restrained and disciplined. Mercury's kisses were always uncontrolled, unrestrained and totally undisciplined.

And heaven help her, but she liked them that way.

In fact, she was liking this kiss so much that when her phone rang, she tried to ignore it, but the persistent ringing had them breaking apart. Still he managed to get in a final lick across her lips before taking a step back.

By the time she pulled the phone from her purse it

had stopped ringing. Just as well, she thought, after seeing the missed call had been from Harold.

Putting her phone back in her purse, she glanced over at Mercury. He was back to staring at her like she was a puzzle he needed to solve. Like he hadn't been the one who'd made the first move to lock lips in a kiss that still had her toes tingling.

"Ready to go? I told Mom I would have you back by four," he said, breaking the silence between them.

"Did you?"

"Yes, and I'm a man of my word."

A man of your word? Let's see about that. "Then will you give me your word that you won't kiss me again?"

"No. Like I said, I'm a man of my word, Sloan."

Twelve

"Would you like to explain what today was all about?"

Mercury took a sip of his beer. He'd known that would be the first question Jaye asked him when they met for their usual happy-hour drinks at Notorious, a popular nightclub in town. The one thing he liked about this place was that the owner opened its doors three hours ahead of the nighttime crowd. On occasion, Mercury would arrive for happy hour and stay through the night, especially if there was live entertainment. The food and the drinks were great. And so was ladies' night every Tuesday.

"Don't pretend you don't know already. I'm sure one of my brothers has enlightened you."

Jaye chuckled. "Yes, it just so happens I ran into Jonas yesterday evening, and he told me what he'd heard. I'm glad you got your car back, by the way."

"Thanks."

"But still, I was surprised when you walked into the bank this morning to help the woman open an account using your own money. Twenty grand is—"

"Twenty grand. I know," Mercury said, still wanting to believe he'd done the right thing.

"I have to admit she's a looker, so I guess you consider it an investment in future benefits," Jaye said, smiling.

Mercury could understand why Jaye thought that. Other than his brothers, Jaye—whom he'd known since grade school and who had been his roommate in college—knew him better than anyone. In fact, it had been Jaye who'd sent out the SOS to his brothers after Cherae had dumped him.

"I don't plan to collect any future benefits."

Jaye nodded, grinning. "That means you're collecting them already."

"No, it doesn't mean that," Mercury said, annoyed that Jaye knew him so well that he would assume that. "In fact, I don't expect anything from her, sexual favors or otherwise."

The grin suddenly left Jaye's face and he stared at him. "Then I think you need to explain why you deposited twenty grand into a woman's account. A woman you just met yesterday, who was driving your stolen car. And while you're at it, you can explain your reasoning for taking her home to Ms. Eden."

Mercury took another sip of his beer. Had it been anyone other than Jaye, he would have told them he didn't have to explain a damn thing. But with Jaye he did.

"I guess I'll start from the beginning. My version and not Jonas's."

"All right."

It took him longer than he'd expected to cover everything with Jaye, only because Nancy Ormond showed
up trying to get his attention, which he refused to give
her. They'd been involved a few months ago, but he had
immediately dropped her after she began hinting that
her biological clock was ticking. As far as he'd been
concerned, that wasn't his problem, and he'd quickly
removed himself from the situation before she got any
ideas about him being some baby daddy.

"So, let me get this straight," Jaye said, when Mercury had finally finished. "Drew told you to fix the
problem, one you didn't make, I might add…and you
figured the solution was to lay cash on her, buy her a
car and put her in an apartment?"

Mercury knew that sounded kind of crazy, but Jaye
was right. "The money in her account is a loan, and
because she doesn't have any established credit, I had
to put the car and apartment in my name."

"Does she know that?"

"Heck no. She would have had a holy cow, but putting them in my name was the only way she could have
gotten them. She'll be paying me back for the car and
the loan, and the apartment will transfer to her name
after six months."

He took a swig of his beer, then added, "When I
heard Sloan's mother talking to her that way, demanding she marry some prick she didn't even like—who
has a woman he wants as his mistress, I might add—I
knew I had to do something."

"Why?"

Mercury's brows arched. "Why what?"

"Why did you feel you had to do something?"

Mercury rolled his eyes. "Did you not hear anything I said? Were you not listening? The woman was in one messy situation."

Jaye shrugged. "And that was your problem how?"

Mercury stared at Jaye. His friend was not some uncaring ass, which meant he was asking him the question for a reason. He had a feeling Jaye wanted him to think through what he'd done. Jaye was late because Mercury had thought things through and was convinced, no matter how it looked to others, helping Sloan out the way he had was the right thing to do. "I told you, Dad told me to handle it."

Jaye leaned back in his chair. "Be careful, Mercury. From what I saw today, it's obvious Sloan Donahue has a problem with depending on others."

"That might be the case, but when you don't have a penny to your name, you have to start somewhere and accept help when offered." Mercury didn't say anything for a minute. Then he asked, "Is there a reason for the lecture, Jaye?"

Jaye took a swallow of his beer. "Yes. I don't want you to make the same mistake with Sloan Donahue that I made with Velvet."

Mercury noted that Jaye hadn't mentioned Velvet in months, not since she'd moved away last year without telling Jaye where she'd gone. Jaye had been warned that one day Velvet would get tired of being his bedmate instead of becoming his wife.

"Whoa, no comparison. You loved Velvet, although you never admitted you did. I don't do women to fall in love. I do women for sex."

"If you recall, that was once my attitude as well, Mercury."

"No, you never did women, at least not after meeting Velvet. I knew you loved her, Jaye, and *if you recall*," he said, repeating Jaye's earlier words, "I told you that you loved her. But you refused to believe me. For three years you dated Velvet exclusively and still you honestly thought it was only about the sex."

"Hell, Mercury, I realize my mistake and will rectify the problem. Soon."

Mercury lifted a brow. "Soon? Just how are you planning to do that when you have no idea where she is?"

"I do now. A few months ago, I hired a PI to find her. I got a call from him before leaving the office to let me know he's found her."

Mercury sat up in his chair. He'd always liked Velvet, and although falling in love was not his thing, he'd known Jaye had cared for Velvet Spencer deeply, but refused to acknowledge that he had. Hell, everyone had known but Jaye. He'd discovered his feelings too late. "So, where is she?"

Jaye met his gaze. "She's living in a coastal town in Louisiana, an hour away from New Orleans. A place called Catalina Cove."

Mercury didn't say anything for a minute. "I take it you're going to come up with a plan to get her back."

A determined look appeared on Jaye's features. "Yes, and it has to be a good one."

"I agree, man. She gave you plenty of chances and you blew each one."

"Don't remind me." Jaye then glanced at his watch. "It's Thursday night. Aren't you going over to your folks' for dinner?"

Mercury knew this was Jaye's way of changing the subject. "Yes, I'm going."

There was no need to tell Jaye that because Mercury knew Sloan would be there, he wasn't in any hurry to get there. There was something about being around her that made him feel vulnerable for the first time since Cherae had left and he didn't like it one damn bit.

Even now he remembered Sloan's kisses. There were too many when there should not have been any. Yet the way her body felt pressed to his, the way her firm breasts and stiff nipples poked him in the chest and the way her tongue would mate with his were torments he couldn't let go of. And to see her again meant not only remembering, but also being tempted for a repeat performance.

"Mercury?"

He glanced over at Jaye. "Yes?"

"Did you hear what I just said?"

No, Mercury inwardly admitted, he hadn't heard. There was no need to lie about it. "Sorry, my mind was elsewhere. What did you say?"

Normally Jaye would have given him a look that said he knew where Mercury's mind was…which was usually on bedding some woman or another. Instead the look he saw on his best friend's face was one of purposeful resolve.

"I asked if you think you will ever fall in love again."

"No." Mercury's attitude about love might be confusing to some, but it shouldn't be to Jaye. "If you recall, I was the first of my brothers to fall in love and you know what Cherae did. Once you've been burned you have a tendency to stay away from the fire."

"That's what you've been doing all these years? Staying away from the fire?"

"Yes, pretty much."

"Then would you like to explain your attraction to Sloan Donahue? I watched you and it's quite obvious that you're taken with her, although you're trying hard not to be."

Mercury didn't like that Jaye was so damn observant. No need to deny anything. "I'll be okay once I get a handle on things."

"If you say so, but I'm finding that hard to believe. You've only known her for two days, yet…"

"Yet what?"

"You seem smitten."

Smitten? Mercury frowned. "And I think you've lost your mind."

"Possibly, but what I saw today and how you were looking at her when you thought no one was noticing says a lot."

In all honesty, that said more than a lot, Mercury thought. That said too damn much. If Jaye could pick up on how attracted he was to Sloan, then his brothers would, too. Hell, he had a good mind not to show up at his parents' place for dinner tonight. But not doing so meant he would be allowing her to get next to him in a way he couldn't control, and he refused to let that happen.

"I'm leaving," he said, standing and glancing at his watch. There were a couple of stops he had to make, as well as going home to change clothes.

"Okay. Take care."

"And, Jaye?"

His friend looked over at him. "Yes?"

"I'm glad you found Velvet."

Jaye smiled. "Me, too, Mercury. Me, too."

Sloan stared up at the five men standing in front of her. One she knew from yesterday, but the others she did not. The one thing she did know was that they were Mercury's brothers. Four were the husbands of the very friendly women she'd met earlier—Brittany, Stacey, Nicole, who was married to Jonas, and Hunter—who'd arrived early to help Eden with dinner.

For a minute, Sloan had felt like an intruder when the women had shown up, but they, along with Eden, had made her feel right at home. And Eden and Drew's grandkids were to die for. The twins were simply adorable, just like Galen had said they were, and the youngest grand, Stacey and Eli's son, had stolen her heart immediately.

Now Sloan was eyeing the green-eyed men standing in front of her. Their eyes might have come from Eden, but their features belonged to Drew. They were the former "Bad News Steeles" minus one. Namely Mercury, who hadn't arrived yet.

"Sloan, let me introduce my brothers," Galen said, smiling. "In order of ages, this is Tyson, Eli, Jonas and Gannon. Missing is Mercury, but you know him already. He fits between Jonas and Gannon."

Sloan smiled brightly as her gaze moved from one brother to the other. Four of them might be happily married now, but she bet they'd all been pistols before marriage. "It's nice to meet all of you."

"The pleasure is ours," the one named Jonas said. "We heard about your misfortunes and we're glad the folks were here to help."

"Thanks, and Mercury helped, too," she quickly said. "If it hadn't been for him, I would not have met your parents."

Eli smiled. "Then we need to commend our brother for acting the part of a hero for once in his life."

As far as Sloan was concerned, Mercury *was* a hero.

"Speaking of Mercury, where is he?" Gannon asked, glancing down at his watch.

"He's late and Mom doesn't like us to show up late. Then she thinks you only come for the meal," Tyson tacked on, grinning.

"Someone's looking for me?" a deep voice said behind Sloan.

She not only recognized the husky tone, but a sudden jolt of sexual energy in the atmosphere had announced his presence. She turned and saw him. He'd changed from the business suit he'd been wearing earlier and was now dressed in a pair of jeans and a white shirt. He looked relaxed and handsome. In the jeans and shirt, his body was hard and muscular, and she was fully aware of the length of him. All his brothers were tall, but he was taller. Only Gannon, the youngest brother, was a wee bit taller.

"Yes, we were looking for you. We said you played the role of hero for Sloan and that was good," Tyson said.

"Only after I reminded him that Mom expected us to treat ladies with the utmost respect, and if there's ever one in need, we're there for the rescue," Galen said.

"Whatever." Mercury switched his gaze to her. "Good evening, Sloan. I hope my brothers aren't boring you to tears."

She chuckled. "No, I'm enjoying their company."

"In fact, I was just about to ask her if she'd like to take a stroll in Mom's courtyard so I can show her all the different types of flowers she has growing there," his brother Gannon said, smiling.

Mercury came to stand by Sloan's side. "No need. I gave Sloan a tour of the courtyard yesterday." He then turned to her. "I need to talk to her about something."

"What about?" Gannon asked, like he had every right to know.

"None of your business."

Sloan was enjoying this playful camaraderie between the brothers. She missed out on this sort of thing by being an only child. It was obvious the six had a fondness for each other, even when they were annoyed.

"Mercury probably has to tell me something about my new car," she said.

Eli lifted a brow. "You got a new car?"

She couldn't help but beam all over the place. "Yes. Hopefully, I'll be picking it up this Friday when I move into my apartment."

"Apartment? You have an apartment?" Tyson asked.

"Yes. I signed a lease as well today, thanks to Mercury."

"Yes, that Mercury is such a nice guy," Galen said, giving his brother a look Sloan couldn't decipher.

"Of course I am. Just like you said, Mom raised us well. Respect and rescue, right?" Mercury said, giving his brother a huge smile.

"I'll be glad to help you move into your apartment," Gannon offered, taking a sip of his before-dinner drink.

"No need—I'm taking care of Sloan."

She wasn't sure she liked the implications of that, but

knew Mercury hadn't meant it the way it sounded and she figured his brothers probably knew that, as well.

"We'll see you guys in the dining room in a minute. Like I said, I have something to discuss with Sloan," Mercury said before presenting his arm to her.

She took it and he escorted her toward his mother's office. The same one where they'd shared a kiss last night. He didn't say anything until he'd closed the door behind him.

"What's going on, Mercury?" she asked him.

After that kiss they'd shared last night and the two they'd shared today, she was somewhat nervous about being alone with him. He had a tendency to make her body feel things.

"I need to give you this," he said, reaching into his jeans pocket and pulling out a phone. "It's a burner. We didn't have time to pick one up today, so I made a stop by the store on my way here."

Getting one had been on her list of things to do. "Thanks. I appreciate you doing that for me. Please be sure to add the cost to the amount I owe you already. It seems I'm getting further and further into your debt, Mercury," she said, sliding the phone into the pocket of her skirt.

"No, you're not. And here's the number to it," he said, handing that to her, as well. "And there's something else you need to know."

She lifted a brow. "What?"

"Your ex-fiancé is in town."

Of all the things she had expected him to say, that hadn't been it. Harold had told her he was coming to Phoenix, but she hadn't believed him. "How do you know?"

"I have a friend connected to Homeland Security. As a favor, I asked her to let me know the moment his plane landed."

Sloan tried ignoring the fact this particular friend of his was a female. "How did you know he'd planned to come here?"

"I overheard that part of your phone conversation with your mother. I figured that meant he knew where you were."

"Only because my father told him." Anger tore into Sloan. Did Harold have no shame? "I've told him countless times that I won't marry him, so coming here was a waste of his time."

"That might be the case, but he may need to hear it again."

"It won't do any good—trust me. He has it in his head that he can do whatever the hell he wants to do where I'm concerned because he has my parents' blessing."

"Sounds like you have a problem, Sloan. In that case, I'm going to give you the same advice my father always gave his sons while growing up and even after we became men."

"Which is?"

"When there's a problem, first up is to find a solution."

She didn't say anything as she tried to digest his words. Good advice for anyone other than herself. She'd never had to come up with a solution to anything because her parents had always fixed her problems. Instead of helping her, she now saw they'd only been hindering her.

"But what if the solution I come up with is not well-thought-out? And ends up causing more harm than good?" she asked, seriously needing to know. She knew what he'd said was true. Her parents were her problem and she needed to take ownership of how to deal with them.

"It's fine if that happens, Sloan. We're human. We make mistakes. On the other hand, we can go back to the drawing board and start over, make new decisions, find new solutions."

She studied him for a minute. "Was there ever a very important problem you had to find a solution for?" For some reason she had a feeling there was.

He broke eye contact with her to look out a single French door that led outside to his mother's courtyard. Moments later, he glanced back at her. "Yes, there was. Finding the solution was difficult, but I did it and I'm glad I did. Taking ownership of the problem fell on me and I'm glad I made the decision that I did."

She nodded, wondering what had been the problem and the solution. It wasn't any of her business and he wasn't sharing any details. "What if my decision is impulsive?"

He chuckled smoothly. "It can happen that way. I call them temporary fixers. But even coming up with something temporary is better than not doing anything. Never let anyone know how intimidated you might be. No matter who they are. Stand your ground. Let them see you as a strong individual, even when your knees might be shaking. Have confidence in yourself even in the face of not feeling confident. Fake it. Who's to know?"

She tilted her head up and looked at him, studied his features. Handsome? Yes, but there was something else she was seeing. That realization made her smile. "You mentor a lot, don't you?"

She could tell by his expression that her question surprised him, caught him off guard. "What makes you say that?" he asked, leaning back against his mother's desk.

In a way, she wished he hadn't done that. His stance made his jeans stretch tight across a pair of muscular thighs. The same thighs that had rubbed against her today when they'd kissed. Both times. Deep feminine appreciation flowed through her. Her attraction to Mercury was becoming so intense that he could and would be placed on her problematic list. He'd become a distraction as well as a temptation. She didn't need either. As one of her problems, she would have to find a solution to deal with him, as well.

Now she wished several hot, passionate solutions weren't flowing through her mind.

Knowing he was waiting for a response to his question, she shrugged her shoulders. "Not sure. I guess it's not only what you're saying but how you're saying it. Like you've given this sort of advice before."

He gave her a look that made her think he wasn't at all happy that she'd been able to read him. But she had.

"My occupation requires it," he finally said. "I represent a lot of sports figures and sign them up for million-dollar contracts. Some have never seen that much money or dreamed of having it. It can pose problems. People they know and are better off not knowing come out of the woodwork. Most of the guys and women are young, inexperienced and not able to handle the vultures, the opportunists, the problems. I periodically give them pep talks, and when a problem arises, I am there for them.

Not to solve it but to help them solve it themselves. They have to come up with their own solutions."

"And if it's the wrong one?" she asked.

"I tell them to never come up with a solution that's not reversible."

A slight frown burrowed between her brows. "So, in other words, no solution should be permanent," she said, trying to follow him.

"Remember permanent means permanent. Ask yourself if that's what you want. And if the solution you come up with seems unconventional, but it will work at the time, there is nothing wrong with doing it to give yourself time to come up with a bigger, more conventional and better plan."

She nodded. He'd certainly given her food for thought. "Thanks, Mercury. I appreciate you sharing your thoughts with me."

"No problem." He moved away from the desk and slowly walked toward her. She met his gaze and could see the same look he normally had right before he would kiss her. And she had a feeling that was his intent now.

They hadn't argued, nor were they at odds with each other like all those other times. If he kissed her, it wouldn't be driven by anything other than desire. Plain and simple.

He came to a stop directly in front of her. He glanced down at her outfit. A flowing skirt and sleeveless blouse with sandals on her feet. When he glanced back at her, he said, "Did I tell you how nice you look?"

"No."

"Then let me do that right now. You look nice, Sloan."

She couldn't help but smile at the compliment. "Thank you, Mercury."

He stared down at her for a moment. Was she imagining things or was his gaze centered on her lips? Evidently her lips thought so because she could feel them start to tingle. Nervous, she swiped her tongue across her bottom lip, then watched how his eyes seemed to lock on the movement.

"I guess we need to get back. We wouldn't want to be the ones holding up dinner, right?" she asked, barely able to get the words out.

He reached up and tucked a strand of hair behind her ear. The movement, the touch, made a shiver run down her spine. As if he'd felt it, his gaze returned to hers and locked in. "You know what I think?"

Why did he ask in that low, husky voice of his? The one that made yet another shiver pass through her.

She swallowed. "No. What do you think?"

"I think they are going to have to wait."

He moved in closer, pressed those tight muscular thighs and firm stomach close to hers and then lowered his mouth to hers. She was so ready and felt a sudden drench of desire invade her the moment his tongue mingled with hers.

Within seconds, it wasn't quite clear whether he was devouring her mouth or she was devouring his. All she knew was that they were taking each other's tongues with a hunger she'd never felt before.

She loved his taste, and from the way he was marauding her mouth, he enjoyed hers, as well. She'd never been kissed like this. Those other times had been hot; however, this was blazing. Now she felt weak in the knees and couldn't help the groan that escaped.

Mercury then ended the kiss with the same intensity he'd used to start it. She appreciated how he wrapped his arms around her, holding her as if to keep her from melting at his feet. The man had practically kissed her senseless and she had no shame in inwardly admitting that she'd liked it.

It took her a minute to catch her breath, take in the scent of him in her nostrils. She thought she could stay like this, being held by him forever, but knew in reality, she couldn't.

Slowly, she lifted her head and met his gaze. He was staring down at her with an odd look on his face. If he was deciding she was a problem just like she'd begun to think he was becoming one, then he would have to follow his own advice and find a solution. She couldn't and wouldn't help him. She had her own issues to deal with. That made her recall what had brought them into his mother's office in the first place.

"Just because Harold is in town doesn't mean he'll be able to find me, right?"

He held her gaze. "Not sure. That would depend on whether or not your father had a tracker on your phone."

His words made her frown. He did. She'd forgotten about that tracker, which at the time her father had said he'd had installed for security reasons. It hadn't mattered to her when she'd left Cincinnati because she hadn't been trying to keep her whereabouts a secret. At least at first she hadn't. Then after her mother's phone call, leaving Phoenix and hiding out somewhere had been her plan until Mercury had pretty much talked her out of it. He was right; it was time she stood her ground and came up with a solution. Even if it was a temporary solution.

"It doesn't matter if Harold eventually finds me. Nothing has changed. We aren't getting married."

Mercury nodded. "I still don't understand why your father would want you to marry him."

She shrugged. "I told you—it's all about merging the two families' wealth. Thanks to an inheritance from my grandfather, when I turn thirty I will come into a large sum of money as well as a bunch of real estate in Texas."

He nodded and took her hand in his. "Come on. Tonight, I want you to forget about your problems. Instead I want you to enjoy the Steele family."

She thought that was a nice thing to say. "Thanks, Mercury. I appreciate you sharing your family with me."

Thirteen

Mercury kept his eyes on Sloan through most of dinner. Memories of the kiss they'd shared were affecting him in ways he hadn't counted on. It didn't take much to recall how easily his tongue had slid between her lips and she'd sucked on his tongue just as greedily as he'd sucked on hers.

He'd heard her moans and was certain he'd released a groan or two himself. But that was fine with him, although he wasn't one who would usually lose control while kissing a woman. Sloan was making it obvious she was different, and he was having a hard time pinpointing just what that difference was.

There was just something about her he found fascinating and it was more than how easily she'd blended in with his family. Everyone liked her; that much was obvious. His parents, his brothers and sisters-in-law and even his niece and nephews.

Even now the look in her eyes was brimming with the kind of happiness he had a feeling she hadn't experienced much, hanging out with a family who loved each other. That didn't mean they all thought alike or got along 100 percent of the time, but it did mean they respected each other's opinions, even when they didn't agree with them. It also meant that, when the time came, they would have each other's backs and would be there for each other.

His only problem with his mom right now was that she had separated him and Sloan. The dining-room table that seated twenty-four was big and long, to accommodate their growing family. Eden had placed him at one end of the table and Sloan at the other. And she'd seated Sloan beside Gannon—the charmer, of all people.

Growing up, Gannon had been in awe of his older brothers. He'd been very impressionable, and their mother had warned them to set positive examples for their youngest brother to follow. With such a tall order, Mercury and his brothers had tried to be low-key around Gannon, but when it came to women, he'd turned out to actually be the worst of the lot. In fact, Gannon always said he was waiting for the day Mercury bit the bachelor dust so he could have all the single ladies in Phoenix to himself.

That was one of the reasons Mercury was keeping an eye on Sloan, to make sure she wasn't being taken in by Gannon's charm. It was obvious his brother was laying it on thick and the two were getting much too friendly to suit Mercury.

"You okay, Merk?"

Mercury turned to Jonas. Whereas all the other

brothers had at least a year and a few months in their ages between them, that wasn't the case for him and Jonas. In fact, for three days they were the same age. Because they were so close in age, there had always been a special bond between them.

"Yes, I'm fine. Why do you ask?"

"Because you've been unusually quiet, and you've been staring at Sloan quite a bit."

"Have I?"

"Yes. By the way, I like her."

He took a sip of his lemonade, then asked in a low voice, "How can you like her when you don't even know her?"

Jonas chuckled and lowered his voice, as well. "I can ask you the same thing."

Mercury frowned. "Who said I liked her?"

"Your mouth. The one that was slightly swollen earlier. So was hers. That means the two of you did some heavy-duty kissing while locked up in Mom's office. I doubt I'm the only one who noticed. So, do you like her?"

Mercury didn't say anything because at that moment Sloan caught his attention when she laughed at something Gannon said. He glanced down the long table at her, and as if she sensed him staring, she looked at him. Their gazes locked and held. There was no way Jonas wasn't noticing, as well as Gannon. Hell, others were probably noticing as well, but he was too mesmerized to care.

Then Drew spoke and Mercury glanced over at his dad. "A game is on tonight. Anyone care to watch?"

His brothers all said yes. Mercury didn't say anything because although he'd dropped eye contact with

Sloan, he was still reeling. While holding her gaze he had tuned out everything around him…except for her.

Jonas leaned over toward him. "You still didn't give me an answer to my question, Merk. But then, you truly don't have to."

"He doesn't have to do what?"

That question had come from Gannon. Mercury then noticed that his brothers were standing around him at the table and everyone else was gone. "Where's Sloan?"

"In the kitchen with Mom and our wives," Galen said, looking at him funny.

"And why are you asking about Sloan?" Gannon asked, grinning. "You need to discuss something else with her locked in Mom's office?"

Mercury frowned. Before he could say anything, Tyson's wife, Hunter, walked into the dining room to grab the plates off the table. It wasn't that he, his brothers or their dad were sexist. They could and did take their own plates to the kitchen, but those were Eden's rules. Thursday was the one night she liked pampering her husband and sons.

When Hunter left, Mercury said, "Let's speak Russian." Because Eden had been a world traveler while modeling, it had been important to her that her sons spoke different languages. That was why Mercury and his brothers had the ability to speak several foreign languages fluently. The last thing he wanted was for Sloan to walk in to discover she was being discussed.

"Fine," Eli said, dropping down in a chair.

Before they could begin their conversation, Sloan entered the room to gather the place mats. She smiled at them and they smiled back. She would probably wonder why they were speaking another language, but knowing she didn't understand them was the important thing.

"We want to know where you stand with Sloan. We don't want her to be taken advantage of," Galen said, starting off the conversation in Russian.

Mercury stared at his brothers. Why did they think he owed them an explanation about anything concerning Sloan? Besides, hadn't it been Eli and Tyson who'd dropped by his office yesterday, all but telling him he needed to do something before Eden got any ideas in her head? He took the time to remind them of that.

"We know," Tyson said. "But that was before we got the chance to meet Sloan. We like her. In fact, we like her a lot. We all do."

"I told you that you would," Galen said, smiling. "She's special."

Mercury tried listening to his brothers while watching Sloan. Damn, she looked good moving around the table gathering the place mats. And she looked like she belonged here.

Belonged here? He didn't like thinking that.

"So, what are your intentions toward her?" Gannon asked. "If you're not going to make a move, I will."

"The hell you will," Mercury said to his youngest brother. "So, back off."

Sloan glanced over at them with concern in her features. Mercury figured that although she couldn't understand what they were saying, she could probably tell he was upset. "Look, guys, we will finish this discussion later," he said, refusing to discuss Sloan with his brothers any longer. At least he'd let Gannon know she was off-limits.

At that moment the doorbell rang. Mercury glanced

over at his brothers. "It's late for visitors. Are the folks expecting anyone?" he asked them, still speaking Russian.

"Not sure," Galen stated. "I'll let Mom know she has company."

"I can do that, Galen," Sloan said. "I need to carry these place mats to the kitchen anyway. You guys can continue on with your conversation." She then left the dining room.

Mercury and his brothers watched her leave, staring at her in shock and feeling the need to pick their jaws up off the floor. She had spoken in fluent Russian. That meant she had not only heard their conversation but had understood every single thing they'd been saying about her.

"Did you know she spoke Russian?" Tyson asked him when they were able to speak.

Still in shock, Mercury shook his head no. The only words he could mutter at that moment were "Ahh hell."

"Eden, someone is at the door," Sloan said, returning to the kitchen.

"Oh? Thanks. I hadn't heard the doorbell," Eden said, wiping her hands on a dish towel before leaving the kitchen.

The other women continued their talk about the latest in fashion and makeup, but Sloan was having a problem contributing. She wished she could put the conversation she'd heard between Mercury and his brothers out of her mind, but she couldn't. Because they'd assumed she didn't understand Russian, they'd felt safe talking about her. At least she knew Mercury's brothers liked her, but he never said whether he did or not.

"Sloan?"

She glanced up to see Eden had returned. "Yes?"

"There's a young man here to see you and he says he's your fiancé."

Harold was here? Mercury had warned her that he could possibly track her in Phoenix, but she honestly hadn't thought he would. He had a lot of nerve coming here. Anger consumed her. "Where is he?"

"I left him in the living room."

"Do I need to go get Mercury?" Eli's wife, Stacey, asked nervously.

Sloan shook her head. "No, I've got this." She walked out of the kitchen and headed toward the living room.

It didn't take her long to get there. Harold seemed to be standing in the middle of it and he looked annoyed. She was grateful the women hadn't followed her. This would be a conversation she and Harold needed to have alone. It was embarrassing enough that he had shown up here. "What are you doing here, Harold?"

He glanced over at her and frowned. "I'm glad your father had a tracker on your phone, or I would not have been able to find you. I called him and he texted me directions straight here."

Agitated, Sloan asked him again, "What are you doing here?"

He had the nerve to smile. "That's obvious. I came for you. I told you that I would. We have a wedding to plan in Cincinnati."

"No, we don't. I told you that. The wedding is off. You should not have come."

He stared at her. "The wedding is on and we're getting married in August."

"Is everything okay, Sloan?"

Hearing the deep voice, Sloan turned to find Mercury, his father and brothers had entered the room. Also, the women. The living room was large enough to accommodate everyone and she didn't resent their presence, but instead felt it was reassuring. In their own way, this family she'd only known for two days was telling her they had her back.

"Yes, Mercury, I'm—"

Before she could finish her response, Harold rudely cut in and said, "Hello, everyone. Thanks for looking out for Sloan, but we have a plane to catch. Her parents have been worried about her."

Sloan wanted to laugh at that. "I'm not going anywhere with you."

Harold had the nerve to chuckle. "Sure you are, sweetheart." He then glanced around at everyone. "Sorry, I didn't introduce myself. I'm Harold Cunningham of the Cincinnati Cunninghams," he said, as if his name meant something.

"And we're the Steeles. The Phoenix Steeles," someone said behind her, and she recognized the voice as Galen's.

"And I'm Mercury Steele," Mercury said, moving forward, extending his hand to Harold. Sloan wondered why Mercury was acting like a diplomat and being so nice.

Harold shook Mercury's hand, and then Mercury proceeded to introduce Harold to every single person in the room. After doing so, Mercury then said, "Harold, we really do appreciate you coming all the way from Ohio to check on Sloan, but as you can see, she's in good hands. When you return to Cincinnati, please be sure to tell her parents that she's in my care and under my protection."

Harold frowned. "Your care and protection? What's that supposed to mean?"

Mercury didn't answer; instead he glanced over at Sloan. She immediately recalled the conversation they'd had in his mother's office. Harold was her problem and she needed to fix it.

Suddenly, an idea for a temporary fix came into her head. As long as Harold and her parents assumed there was a chance for the marriage to go on, they would keep hounding her. That was what this was about anyway. That was what had driven her away from Ohio. Her parents' insistence that she and Harold marry to expand their families' wealth.

Drawing in a deep breath, Sloan moved to stand beside Mercury. She hoped he recognized what she was about to do as a temporary fix and that he wouldn't fall flat on his face from shock. From the look on his face earlier, finding out she understood Russian had been shocking enough.

She met her ex-fiancé's gaze. "Harold, what it means," she said in a clear voice, "is that..." She paused and gave Mercury a quick please-forgive-me-for-this smile before turning back to Harold. "Mercury is my fiancé and we're getting married. In fact, we were planning our wedding when you showed up. So now will you please leave?"

Fourteen

Sloan had just told a whopper of a lie and for the longest time the entire room got quiet. She hadn't known what to expect, especially from the man standing by her side whom she refused to look at. Instead her attention was trained on Harold.

She watched the expression on his face show shock and then outrage. Outrage? Honestly? The man who'd told her his mistress would become a permanent part of their lives?

Then Harold spoke. "Don't be ridiculous, Sloan. How can you be engaged to him when you are engaged to me?"

"I *was* engaged to you, but if you recall, I broke off our engagement weeks ago."

"And now you're going to marry a man you barely know?"

"Why not? I thought I knew you and found out I truly didn't." She hated that the Steeles were privy to this conversation, but she wouldn't let that stop her.

"Your parents won't approve of you marrying anyone but me," Harold had the nerve to boast.

She lifted her chin and stiffened her spine. "Then it's a good thing I'm not seeking their approval."

Harold rubbed his hand down his face. "Do you know what will happen to the Donahues and Cunninghams without your...?"

His voice trailed off and she wasn't sure if it was because he suddenly realized they had an audience or if perhaps there was something else. "My what?"

Harold quickly shoved his hands into his pockets. "Nothing."

Yes, there was something and she was determined to find out what it was. "Let's be honest, Harold. You don't love me and I don't love you. In fact, you told me that you want the woman you do love to be a part of our marriage and I refused that."

Sloan's last statement caused a gasp from the back, she wasn't sure from whom, but she didn't care that all the Steeles knew why she'd ended her engagement. "What you do is your business," she continued. "But I won't allow myself to be manipulated by my parents any longer. I will have the freedom to choose the man I want in my life and not the one they want for me. I suggest you do like I'm doing and be your own person and marry who you want. Money isn't everything."

Harold was quiet for a minute and then he said in a somewhat subdued tone, "I need to speak with you privately. There's something you need to know."

A part of Sloan wanted to tell him that there was

no room for further discussion, but a pleading look in his eyes stopped her. She would listen to whatever he said, and then she would tell him to leave and stay out of her life. "Fine. We'll talk privately." She then turned to Eden and Drew. "May I use your office?"

Eden nodded. "Certainly."

"And as your *fiancé*, I intend to be a part of this *private* discussion," Mercury said, meeting her gaze.

Sloan would rather he wasn't. However, considering that she'd given him the title of fiancé without his permission… She didn't want to think how he was feeling about that. She just hoped he remembered their discussion about solutions, and that what she'd done was a temporary fix.

"I'd rather you weren't," Harold said curtly.

"Doesn't matter. That's the way it's going to be," Mercury said.

"Mercury is right, Harold. He can be privy to whatever you have to tell me since he knows all of my business anyway," she said, suddenly realizing just how true that was.

"Okay," Harold said tersely.

"This way." Taking her hand, Mercury led her toward his mother's office and Harold followed.

"So, what do you want to talk to Sloan about, Cunningham?" Mercury asked, leaning back against the door.

He was trying to reel in emotions that were swamping him. He wasn't sure what was upsetting him the most, finding out Sloan had understood his and his brothers' conversation in Russian earlier, Stacey coming down into the dining room to announce it was Sloan's fiancé at the door, or Sloan's lie that he was her fiancé.

He had wanted her to fix her problem with Cunningham but claiming Mercury was her fiancé was not what he'd had in mind.

Sloan had taken a seat on the sofa and Harold had the nerve to sit on the sofa, as well. At least the man had the decency to make sure there was space between them.

Instead of answering him directly, Harold shifted in his seat and turned to Sloan. "I don't think you understand how important a marriage between us is to your father."

"Then tell me, Harold."

Harold shot a look over at Mercury before looking back at her. "I honestly wish we could speak privately."

"That won't be happening," Mercury said, meaning every word.

Sloan glanced over at him and then back at Harold. "Mercury is right, so please answer. Why is a marriage between us so important, other than combining the families' wealth?"

Harold didn't say anything for a minute. "I think your father needs a lot of capital for some reason. I overheard a private conversation between my father and yours regarding your trust fund. The one left to you by your grandfather."

Sloan frowned. "Why would our fathers be discussing my trust fund?"

"Your father wants us to marry so they can get their hands on it."

Sloan shook her head. "That's not possible. I can't get my trust fund until I'm thirty."

"I suggest you verify that, Sloan. I gather from the conversation I overheard that might not be the case.

And you, of all people, know your father. Whatever he wants, he gets. He has friends in high places. He could financially ruin these people who've helped you. Do you want that?"

"Stop trying that scare tactic, Cunningham," Mercury said, having heard enough. "Her father can't ruin my family financially. But we could ruin him. Maybe you need to let him know that."

Harold stared at Mercury and he stared back for the longest moment. Then Harold said, "And I will certainly tell him."

"Good."

Harold stood. "You've been forewarned."

Mercury moved away from the door for Harold to walk out. There was no doubt in his mind that one, or possibly all, of his brothers would escort Cunningham to the door with a warning to never come back.

"Are you okay, Sloan?"

She glanced up at him and he could see the hurt in her eyes. "Yes, I'm okay. Sorry that I used you as my temporary fix."

He nodded. "It took me a minute to figure out that's what you were doing. I'm okay with it for now." He needed to let her know he expected her to start working on a permanent solution, but for some reason he let it go.

"I need to talk to your parents. Your family. I owe them an apology for Harold even showing up here tonight like he did and for having to listen to our issues. I feel embarrassed."

"Don't feel that way," he said, easing down beside her. "I'm sure you know by now that my family likes you, and we are here for you, no matter what."

Mercury could tell his words touched her and she was about to get emotional. He wasn't used to emotional women. For a moment he felt out of his element. Then he recalled Eli saying that he'd learned that emotional women liked to be held, when his wife, Stacey, was very emotional while pregnant. Hell, Mercury didn't hold women; he bedded them and then moved on to the next. If he showed too much empathy, they might get clingy. A clingy woman was nothing but trouble.

But for some reason, he felt compelled to give Sloan a little more consideration than he gave to most. Probably surprising her just as much as he was surprising himself, he reached over and swooped her into his arms and placed her in his lap. Then he wrapped his arms securely around her.

When she tilted her head back to look up at him, he said, "I figured everyone needs a little cuddling every once in a while, and I would be the first to admit that the last two days have been pretty damn hellish for you."

"Will they get better, Mercury?"

He released a soft chuckle that was meant to charm her. He wasn't sure why, when he wasn't a charmer like Gannon. "We're going to hope, okay?"

"Okay." And then she placed her head against his chest.

Why it was important to him that she felt safe and secure, he wasn't sure, but it was. For a long moment neither said anything. Then he asked her the one question that was still on his mind. "Sloan?"

"Yes?"

"Why didn't you tell me you speak Russian?"

She glanced up at him, her brow furrowing. "I speak seven different languages."

"Seven?"

"Yes. Besides English, I speak French, Italian, German, Spanish, Russian and Swahili. I assumed you knew, since the job I'm interviewing for is interpreter for the Miss Universe pageant."

Mercury was surprised. "An interpreter for Miss Universe?"

"Yes. What sort of job did you think it was?"

He shrugged. He certainly hadn't thought it would be that. "A traveling companion since Ms. Fowler likes to travel a lot. Mom had mentioned months ago she would be looking for one."

Sloan chuckled. "A traveling companion? I doubt a salary doing that will pay my bills, Mercury."

He'd figured that much, as well. "That job as an interpreter sounds interesting," he said.

She smiled. "I think so, too. I'm excited about the prospect of doing something like that."

She glanced at her watch. "I need to talk to your family. I hope they haven't left yet."

He doubted they had. His brothers and sisters-in-law would want to make sure she was okay before they left. "You don't have to talk to them."

"I want to. I know what you're saying about my father's scare tactics, but your brothers need to be told, as well. Harold is right—my father will try coming after anyone who befriends me."

He stood and placed her on her feet. She tilted her head back to look up at him.

"So, you and your brothers speak Russian, too?" she asked.

"Yes," Mercury said, grinning. "Besides English, we speak Russian, Spanish, German and French."

She nodded. "That's good to know."

They headed for the door, Mercury taking her hand in his. "Yes, that's good to know," he agreed.

Hours later, long after his mother and Sloan had gone to bed and his sisters-in-law and niece and nephews had left to go home, Mercury, his brothers and father were still in his father's man cave. Sloan had apologized to everyone for Harold's unexpected arrival, and like he'd known they would, his family had basically assured her that Harold's surprise appearance hadn't bothered them. She'd also told them about what a tyrant her father could be and that he had no qualms about going after anyone who would help her defy him. They'd pretty much told her to let him try.

Drew stood. "I assume you have a plan, Mercury?"

Mercury couldn't help but chuckle. "Yes, Dad, I have a plan."

"You're marrying her, right?" Galen asked, grinning.

Mercury frowned. "No. I'm not marrying anyone. Her claiming that I was her fiancé was just a temporary fix. She knows she has to come up with a permanent solution…but in the meantime, this is what I propose."

His brothers all leaned toward him. "What?" Tyson asked.

"I need to call Quade to find out every single thing I need to know about Sloan's father."

Quade Westmoreland was married to their cousin, the former Cheyenne Steele, and lived in Charlotte, North Carolina. For years Quade worked with the PSF, the Presidential Security Forces, dual branches of the Secret Service and CIA. Now he owned an elite PI firm, in addition to a network of security companies around the country and abroad. "We need to know everything about the man we're dealing with."

Everyone nodded their agreement. Quade would leave no stone unturned and his report would be thorough. Mercury then said, "I also need to find out more about Sloan's trust fund. You heard what she told us tonight. She honestly doesn't know much about it. All she knew was that she would get it whenever she turned thirty."

Mercury looked over at Eli. "Since Sloan hired you as her attorney tonight, what do you plan on doing?"

"I'm meeting with Sloan here in the morning to get more information," he said. "Specifically, I need the name of her grandfather's attorney. Then I'll be contacting him and go from there."

"That sounds like a plan," Mercury said.

"When is Sloan moving into her apartment?" Jonas asked. "Will it be safe for her to do that? I hate to say it but her parents sound like a pair of loonies."

Gannon laughed. "You can go ahead and say it because they do."

Mercury smiled and shook his head, but Gannon was right. They did. "Sloan's moving into her apartment tomorrow. The place is already furnished, so all she has to do is move in. Just to be on the safe side, I'll hang around her more often."

"More often than you do now?" Gannon asked with a smirk on his face.

Ignoring his youngest brother's comment, Mercury said, "I'll contact Quade first thing in the morning."

Fifteen

Sloan glanced across the breakfast table at Eli with an apologetic look on her face. "I'm sorry, Eli, but I don't have the answer to any of those questions. The only reason I know the name of my grandfather's attorney is because I met him a few times."

Eli nodded, pushing his folder aside. "And you don't think he's been corresponding with your parents on your behalf?"

"I would think not. Charles Rivers and my grandfather were close. I recall his father was my grandfather's friend for years, and when Mr. Rivers finished law school, he became Pop's private attorney. He knew how my grandfather felt about my parents meddling in his affairs."

"Did your grandfather know the Cunninghams?"

Sloan shrugged her shoulders. "Not that I know of.

At least he never mentioned them to me. In fact, I'm almost sure he didn't. If I recall, the Cunninghams and my parents became friends after my grandfather passed away, when they moved their company to Cincinnati."

"Hopefully, I'll be able to reach out to Charles Rivers today," Eli said, standing. "I understand you're moving into your own place today."

Sloan couldn't help the bright smile that touched her lips. "Yes, I am. And my new car is being delivered today, as well. I am so excited. Mercury is arriving around noon and I'm all packed and ready to go."

"I'll let you know if I hear anything from Rivers."

"Thanks."

A few hours later, Sloan was prepared to leave when Mercury arrived. Giving both Drew and Eden hugs, she thanked them for their generous hospitality and told them she would be inviting them to her place when she got settled. "When will my car be delivered?" she asked Mercury excitedly, as they drove away from his parents' home.

"It should be there by the time we arrive at your apartment."

"My apartment. I like the sound of that." She truly did. While living with her parents, she'd never given any thought to moving out since she basically had her own wing of the house and nobody monitored her comings and goings. At least she hadn't given leaving any thought until she'd had enough.

She glanced over at Mercury. He was wearing a nice suit. "You went to work today?"

"Yes, this morning. I had a couple of meetings. I try to wrap up things by lunchtime on Fridays to get a head start on my weekend."

"Big plans?"

"The usual."

She wondered what was the usual for him, but knew not to ask. What he did and with whom was his business. She should appreciate the time he'd given her the last two days and let it go.

But a part of her couldn't help remembering how when she'd gotten upset last night about Harold's appearance and the entire situation with her father, Mercury had placed her in his lap and held her.

She couldn't ever remember anyone doing that for her before. And the sad thing was that she'd needed it. She hadn't known just how much until he'd performed the selfless act.

"Nikki and Hunter will be dropping by later to bring over toiletries and stuff I might need. I think it's nice of them to do that."

"I have a nice family. By the way, how did your meeting with Eli go this morning?"

"I think it went okay." She spent the next twenty minutes filling him in on everything.

"Eli is a good attorney. And just so you know, I have a family member who used to work for the CIA checking out a few things on your father."

"CIA? That's a little deep, don't you think? Trying to keep me under their control is nothing like selling government secrets to other countries," she said, making light of her situation.

"You never know what motivates people to do what they do, Sloan."

"I know what motivates my parents, Mercury. Money. My grandfather would say that all the time." Not wanting to talk about her parents any longer, she told Mercury about her to-do list and how glad she was to have a car to get around town.

"So, what are your plans for the weekend?" he then asked her.

"I'm going to relax, maybe check out that mall on the corner and buy a book to read. Your mother invited me to church with her on Sunday. I figured I'd do some interview practice sessions Sunday evening for my talk with Ms. Fowler."

"Interview practice sessions?"

"Yes. Although she's not doing the official hiring for the pageant, I understand that if she recommends me for the position, then there's a good chance I'll get it. I want to make a good impression on her."

"You will. Just be yourself."

Moments later, they were pulling into her apartment complex and she drew in a huge, exhilarated breath. This would be her place. Granted, she didn't own it, but it would be hers nonetheless. The apartment would be her home.

"You okay?"

She smiled over at Mercury. "Yes, I'm okay. I couldn't be better."

Mercury stood in the living room and watched Sloan slowly walk around, moving from room to room, as if she was in awe. If truth be known, he was in total awe of her. Today she was attired in another sundress, this one a beautiful floral print. Her hair was swept up with a few loose strands framing her face. Her makeup was never heavy, always soft and subtle and barely looked as if she was wearing any.

He'd had to mentally prepare himself to see her

again today, after having thought about her into the wee hours of the morning. When had he thought about another woman as much? Hell, he doubted he ever had. He'd tried convincing himself it was because of her ex-fiancé's visit last night. The man had had a lot of gall to show up at the Steeles' home.

Then there was that moment between Mercury and Sloan afterward in his mother's office when he'd placed her in his lap and held her. It was during that time that he'd felt emotions that were so unlike him. Totally uncharacteristic. Atypical. She had the ability to make him behave like a totally different guy. Like now.

Drawing in a deep breath, Mercury knew there was no reason for him to still be here. She was in her apartment and had a car, which meant his services were no longer needed. He should be on his way to Notorious to get an early start on the weekend and check the lineup of women who were probably already there. Ready for some action, a one-night stand, a Mercury quickie or a Mercury Steele seduction.

Yet he was still here, watching her, staring as she strolled from room to room, admiring her beauty. He loved the size of her breasts and the shape of her thighs, easily displayed whenever she moved. There was a gracefulness about her stride. He figured she'd probably attended one of those finishing schools, and that was the reason she and Galen's wife, Brittany, had hit it off last night. But then, Sloan had impressed everyone without even trying to do so.

He'd meant what he'd told her in the car. When she met with Ms. Fowler on Monday she should just be herself. There was something about her that drew people in. His brothers, parents and sisters-in-law had been drawn in immediately. It had taken a little longer for him, only because of their rocky beginning. But now he was all in, and like the rest of the Steeles, he was Team Sloan.

She stopped walking, turned and gave him a smile that heightened his pulse and made a hard hum of lust flare through his veins. Her smile and his reaction to it had been so unexpected he'd immediately shifted, feeling weak in the knees. Otherwise, he might have fallen flat on his face.

What was he thinking? No woman could make him fall flat.

"Tell me about *your* apartment, Mercury."

Why did she want to know about his apartment? Usually when a woman asked about his apartment, that meant she was hinting at an invitation. However, he doubted that was the case with Sloan. "What would you like to know about it?"

"Although this place is furnished, I'm still considering decorating ideas. Nothing costly. Definitely within my budget."

He liked how she was forever mindful of her budget, trying hard not to overspend. He knew that would be something she would have to get used to since that hadn't been her way of life before now. "Unlike these white walls, mine are colorful."

"Colorful?"

"Yes. It wasn't my choice. I hired a decorator and told her to do her own thing. Unfortunately, she was into bold colors. It took me a while to get used to them, but now I can't imagine my walls any other way."

She tipped her finger to her chin and glanced around, as if thinking about it. Why did seeing her doing something so mundane look sexy as hell? He bet she would be hot in bed.

He forced back a groan, knowing he shouldn't be thinking of Sloan in a sexual way. But he had and this wasn't the first time he'd done so. And why not? She was a woman. He was a man. He'd already admitted to their attraction by kissing her. And they had been kisses he'd totally enjoyed. Kisses he'd gone to bed thinking about. Kisses that were becoming greedier and more erotic every time they shared them.

What had Jonas told him at dinner last night? It had been obvious to everyone that Mercury and Sloan had been kissing when they walked out of his mother's office because their lips were swollen. For that to happen had meant some heavy-duty kissing had gone down behind those closed doors. He would admit it had.

Normally, if he was attracted to a woman, he would have made several home runs by now. With Sloan, he hadn't even tried swinging. He'd been satisfied with going to the bat with the kisses. He'd figured she had too many issues for him. Issues he didn't want to become involved with.

Now, that was a laugh since he was involved. All the way up to his balls.

And speaking of his balls…

They were actually twitching with need for her. He could just imagine that same finger that was tapping her chin stroking them, cupping them before using that same hand to feel him all over. Just the thought of her touching him down there—hell, touching him anywhere—had him feeling the area behind his zipper expand. He needed to leave. Now.

"I've got to go," he said, moving toward the door.

"There's an important appointment I need to keep. I'll see you later."

And then he was gone.

He walked quickly to his car without looking back. In fact, he nearly held his breath until he reached his car, got inside and buckled his seat belt. When had he rushed away from a woman's place instead of rushing to it? Okay, he did remember rushing from Nancy Ormond's place the night she hinted at wanting him to father her baby. That was an altogether different issue than what had him dashing from Sloan's apartment.

He checked his watch and decided that he would go home and change clothes, chill a bit and then hit Notorious. He needed a night in some woman's bed. There had been a woman he'd seen last night when he'd been there with Jaye. She had given him the eye and had even flirted with him when he'd been about to leave. Maybe he'd be lucky and hit the jackpot tonight.

In fact, he intended for that to happen.

Sixteen

Yippee! She had the job!

Sloan was tempted to do a happy dance around her apartment, but she didn't want to disturb the Hollisters, the couple living in the apartment below her. She had met them when she'd gone bike riding on Sunday. Of all things, she had purchased a bicycle on Saturday. She loved her blue bike and went riding every morning.

She thought about the phone call she'd just received. After their talk yesterday, Margaret Fowler had been so taken with Sloan that she'd immediately called the pageant committee to put in a good word for her. Yesterday evening they had called to arrange a Skype interview that she'd thought had gone well. Obviously it had, since she'd just received a call from the pageant's hiring team, who'd said the job was hers.

She had been blown away by the salary they'd offered. It was more than Sloan had thought it would be. Nearly three times as much. They'd explained it was based on the number of languages she spoke. That meant she would be able to pay Mercury back sooner than planned for the loan, and hopefully she could double up on her car payments and pay the bank off sooner, as well.

Mercury...

Sloan hadn't seen or talked to him since Friday, when he'd brought her here. She had gone to church with members of his family on Sunday. After church she'd been invited to Galen's home in the mountains for dinner. She'd figured Mercury would show up, but he hadn't. She didn't want to admit to being disappointed at not seeing him, but she was. It was Tuesday and he still hadn't called. Not even to say hello and see how she was doing.

She wished she could talk to him to tell him about her new job, her *first* job, and she was excited about it. She refused to let Mercury's absence rain on her parade. She wouldn't call him. Chances were, he felt he'd spent too much time with her already and wanted his life back, the way it was before meeting her.

Fine, she hoped he was enjoying it. She couldn't let his absence get to her. Besides, she had plenty to keep her busy. She needed to set up her office since she would begin working from home in a few weeks. The laptop she owned was old and it was time to upgrade to a more advanced model. Then she would need a printer that had both scanning and faxing capabilities. She also needed to purchase office supplies.

However, Sloan knew no matter how busy she was, she would think about Mercury. She thought about him when she woke up every morning and he took over her dreams when she went to sleep at night. Those two days they'd spent together had meant everything to her. Evidently more to her than to him. Undoubtedly those kisses had been no different than any others he'd shared with women. They'd meant nothing to him and probably didn't even compete.

No surprise, since she had limited experience when it came to men. Harold hadn't wanted to make love to her and now she knew why. And that one time with Carlos Larson had been a total waste of time. Probably not for him, but definitely for her. She'd been wholly disappointed. Sloan had a feeling a night with Mercury would not disappoint her.

A night with Mercury...

She shouldn't be thinking such things even after four kisses and a cuddling session in his lap. He'd only indulged her as his way to either chastise, comfort or talk sense into her. His methods were effective and quite enjoyable.

The ringing of the doorbell meant she had a visitor. Other than the Hollisters, who lived downstairs, the only people who knew where she lived were the Steeles. She tried ignoring the tingling sensation in her stomach at the possibility that it could be Mercury.

She checked the peephole and couldn't see the person's face for the huge green plant in front of it. Could it be Mercury? Swallowing deeply, she asked, "Who is it?"

She then held her breath. Hoping. Wishing. Wanting it to be...

"It's Gannon, Sloan. I brought you a housewarming gift."

She let out the breath she'd been holding and with it came deep disappointment. What had she expected? Had her claiming he was her fiancé made him want to put distance between them? That had to be it, although he seemed to have accepted her explanation as to why she'd done it. Had he given it further thought and decided he didn't want her to get any ideas about where their relationship was going or wasn't going? The bottom line was they didn't even have a relationship.

That had to be it. What else could it be? Was keeping his distance a way of making sure she understood that?

"Sloan?"

She blinked. Gannon had to be wondering why she hadn't opened the door yet. "Yes. Just a minute."

Pasting a huge smile on her face, she opened the door and said, "Gannon! It's good to see you. Come in. Ahh, this plant is beautiful. Thanks for my gift."

Mercury leaned back in his chair and absently tossed paper clips back and forth in the center of his desk. Then he would gather them all up and start the process all over again. It was an unproductive way to spend his time, but he would do anything to keep his mind off Sloan.

He had deliberately stayed away from her the past four days and intended to add four more. That meant he would be a no-show Thursday night at his parents' for dinner. He wasn't ready to see her and at least he had an alibi. He would be flying out Thursday morning to Dallas for a high school basketball game. His eyes were on a player by the name of Brock Dennison. Brock was only seventeen, which meant he had to complete at least two years of college before he could get signed on with the NBA at nineteen.

Any other time Mercury would be looking forward to such a trip, but he was not this time. Although he knew he should keep putting distance between himself and Sloan, part of him didn't want to. He wanted *her*. Hell, he hadn't even been able to pique his interest for any other woman. He'd gone to Notorious four nights in a row and women had thrown themselves at him; a couple of them had all but invited him out to their cars for quickies, and he'd turned them all down. Granted, he did have discriminating taste, but still, he'd never gone this long without getting laid. So why was he going through self-induced torture?

He knew the reason and had already admitted to it.

He wanted Sloan. And he wanted her bad.

He wanted to seduce the hell out of her, knowing he would enjoy every minute of doing so. However, he'd made up his mind not to cross the line with her. She wasn't one of those women a man would enjoy in bed without wanting more, more and even more. She was the kind of woman a man could get addicted to. Hell, wasn't he addicted to her taste already after just four kisses? He could close his eyes and remember how his tongue felt in her mouth, the lusciousness. Needing to savor the memories, he closed his eyes and remembered sucking her lower lip into his mouth, nipping on it a few times before their tongues dueled in one hell of a heated encounter.

He would seduce her with even more hot, deep and erotic glides of his tongue. More than once he'd been tempted to take her just where they stood and...

The buzzer on his desk had him snapping his eyes

back open. He glanced at the stack of paper clips, scooped them up and placed them in the designated bowl before clicking on the buzzer. "Yes, Pauline?"

"Your brother is here to see you, Mr. Steele."

Mercury frowned. "Which one?" Not that he was in the mood to visit with any of them. No doubt they were here to get in his business, wanting to know why he'd been a no-show at Galen's on Sunday.

"Mr. Gannon Andrew Steele."

Mercury shook his head. His brothers had given up trying to figure out why Gannon wanted to gloat that he'd gotten their father's name. It didn't matter to the five of them since they were all Drew's boys. They had the looks and high testosterone levels to prove it.

"Send him in."

It didn't take long for Gannon to walk through the door, smiling broadly. Mercury wondered what the huge grin was for. "Any reason you're not working today?" he asked his youngest brother, who took a chair without being invited.

"I'm leaving in the morning to make a pickup in Santa Fe and won't be back for a week."

Mercury frowned. "It will take you a week to go to Santa Fe and back?"

Gannon's grin widened. "No."

There was no need to ask Gannon what he would be doing while he was in Santa Fe. Mercury knew it had nothing to do with taking in the sights...unless you counted some woman's bedroom as something to see.

Over forty years ago, Drew Steele had taken his small trucking company and turned it into a million-dollar industry with routes all over the United States. When Drew retired, Gannon had taken over the company as CEO. Gannon enjoyed getting behind the rig himself on occasion and Mercury and his brothers knew why.

"So, what's this I hear about you agreeing to be on the cover of Chloe's magazine?" Mercury asked Gannon. Chloe Westmoreland was someone they considered a cousin-in-law since she was married to Ramsey Westmoreland, who was a cousin to Quade.

Mercury wasn't sure how it was possible, but Gannon's smile got even wider. "I guess Quade told you about that, uh? You know what they say. If you got it, you might as well flaunt it."

And Mercury knew Gannon was convinced he had *it*. "Whatever."

Suddenly the smile disappeared from Gannon's face. "And speaking of Quade, is his firm checking out that business with Sloan?"

"I told you guys last week that I was pulling him in to check out some things for me."

"Yes, and you also said you would be hanging around Sloan more, too, but you haven't been doing it."

Mercury frowned. "I didn't need to. I have a friend who works for Homeland Security constantly checking the airline database. Cunningham left Phoenix, and if Sloan's father shows up in town, I'll know it before his plane lands." He then lifted a brow. "And how do you know what I've been doing or not doing with regard to Sloan?"

"Because I just left her place and she said she hadn't seen you since Friday, the day she moved into her apartment."

Mercury's frown deepened. "What do you mean, you just left Sloan's place? Why were you there?"

Now the smile returned to Gannon's face. A slight one, but one just the same, and it was enough to let Mercury know the last thing he should have done was lose his cool at the thought of Gannon visiting Sloan.

"Any reason you want to know, Mercury?"

"Don't play games with me, Gannon. Why were you at Sloan's apartment?"

Gannon smiled a little more. "Hey. No need to get all jealous. I bought her a housewarming gift that I wanted to take her before I left town."

"I wasn't getting jealous."

Gannon laughed. "You could have fooled me. On the other hand, no, honestly, you can't. You like her and you know it."

Refusing to get baited by his brother, Mercury asked, "How is she?"

"Not telling. If you want to know, then go see her for yourself. But I will tell you this. Although she tried to hide it, I could see the disappointment in her face when she saw it was me and not you."

"You're imagining things."

The smile was off Gannon's face again. "No, I'm not. I suggest you make some decisions, Mercury."

"About what?"

"Not what but who. Sloan. You like her and she likes you. Get to know her or you could lose the best thing to ever happen to you."

Mercury didn't say anything for a long moment. "You know about Cherae."

Gannon rolled his eyes. "Hell, everybody knew about Cherae but you. Stop finding excuses since we all know that Sloan is nothing like her. Cherae was running toward money and Sloan seems determined to run away from it. All she wants is to live as normal a life as possible. On a budget," he said, grinning.

Gannon paused and then added, "And she thinks that car is in her name and that she got the apartment on her own. She's proud of those accomplishments. I think you need to set the record straight before someone else does. The last thing you want is for her to think you played her and cared nothing about her need for independence."

"I wasn't trying to play her, only help her."

"Let her know that. After you tell her, then all she's going to do is add it to the budget to pay you back. I've never known a woman so excited about being on a budget."

Mercury chuckled. "Yes, I know."

"Well, something else you might not know is that she got that job with the Miss Universe pageant. They notified her today and she was extremely happy about it."

"And I'm happy for her."

"Then tell her, Mercury. I believe she would appreciate hearing that from you." Gannon stood. "I'll see you when I get back."

Gannon had made it to the door when he turned back to Mercury. "And just so you know, the thought of me being the lone Bad News Steele doesn't bother me. With you out of the way here, that clears the field for me to have all the women."

"Does it?"

"Sure does. And whenever I visit North Carolina with no more single Steeles there to worry about, and with those Bachelors in Demand finally all married off, I'll be king of the road…if you know what I mean."

Unfortunately, Mercury knew. "Don't rush things with me and Sloan. I might like her, but that doesn't mean I want things to go any further."

Gannon chuckled. "If you honestly think that, then you're only fooling yourself. You were the first of the pack to break away and fall in love with Cherae. That means you're capable of loving a woman, Mercury. All you have to do is let some of that ice thaw from around your heart and you'll be okay."

Mercury couldn't believe his baby brother was actually trying to give him advice or that he was even listening. "For Pete's sake, I've barely known her a week."

"And? If you recall, Galen was trying to convince Brittany to move in with him the same day they met."

Mercury remembered, and he also recalled how the five of them had nearly flipped their lids not only when they heard about it, but also when they'd found out Galen had talked Brittany into agreeing. In the end, Brittany and Galen had fallen in love. "I'm not Galen."

"No, but you are Drew Steele's son. Don't forget Dad almost lost Mom because he was convinced he was not ready to love her or any woman. But look at him now. If Drew hadn't come to his senses, there would not have been any of us. Hell, can you imagine being born to any other parents? Parents like Sloan's?"

Mercury cringed at the thought. "No."

Then without saying anything else, Gannon opened the door and left.

Seventeen

Sloan stood back and admired her work area. She had a new laptop, a new printer, a beautiful green plant—compliments of Gannon—on her desk, and all the office supplies she needed to start her new job, although she wouldn't officially begin working for a few weeks.

Tomorrow she had a mobile conference call with the pageant committee. They wanted to get to know her and wanted her to get to know them. The thought that they'd hired her so quickly based on Margaret Fowler's recommendations meant a lot to her.

It was just a little past eight and dark outside already. She had taken a bubble bath and changed into a pajama shorts set. Next on her list of things to do was to enjoy a glass of wine, compliments of Tyson and Hunter. Jonas and Nikki had given her a beautiful set of wine-glasses, which she couldn't wait to use with the wine.

Galen and Brittany had given her a starter kit of every spice that existed. Since she wouldn't begin work for another month, she figured she could take Mercury's advice and enroll in a cooking class.

Mercury...

Hadn't she told herself she would not think about him today, tomorrow or any other day? The fact that he hadn't called said a lot. She'd been tempted to ask Eden about him, but had talked herself out of doing so.

She was about to go into the kitchen for a glass of wine when her phone rang. She checked caller ID and saw it was Eli. When she'd seen him at Galen's on Sunday, he'd told her he had spoken to Charles Rivers's personal assistant, who said Rivers was out of town and wouldn't be back until Tuesday. Hopefully that meant Eli had talked to him today.

"Yes, Eli?"

"Hello, Sloan. I made a connection with Charles Rivers and I need to discuss with you what he shared. Are you free tomorrow morning? I can drop by your place on my way to the office."

She knew from Stacey that she and Eli lived in a community not far from there. "That would be great. I'm in apartment C240."

"Okay. Will nine o'clock work?"

"Yes, that will be fine."

"Okay, I'll see you in the morning."

"Thanks, Eli."

Sloan had just disconnected the call when she heard the sound of the doorbell. Immediately, there was a pounding in her chest, hoping it was Mercury. Hadn't she just convinced herself that it hadn't mattered if she saw him or not? So why was she having such an intense reaction at the possibility it was him?

Moving to the door, she inwardly told herself that even if it was him, he'd probably only dropped by to deliver the documents for her car and the payment sheet for the loan since she was yet to get them from him.

"Yes? Who is it?"

"Mercury. May I come in?"

He was asking to come in and she hadn't opened the door yet? Erring on the side of caution, she looked out the peephole to verify it was him, although she'd recognized his sexy voice. Releasing a deep breath, she opened the door.

"Hello, Sloan."

She wished he didn't say her name in that strong, husky voice. And more than anything, she wished he wasn't standing in front of her door looking the epitome of masculine beauty in his business suit. Why did he have such chiseled good looks that looked even more so when half lit by the moonlight?

"Mercury," she said, stepping aside. No matter what, she would not ask where he'd been the last four days and what he'd been doing...or with whom. He was the one who'd put distance between them, which meant he had a problem with her.

It was his problem and he was the one who needed to find a solution.

When he walked over the threshold, the scent of his cologne was enough to make her insides shiver. He stopped in front of her and that was when she saw the package he was holding. "This is a housewarming gift for you."

She looked down at the prettily wrapped white box with a sky blue bow. "Thank you, Mercury."

"You're welcome."

He stepped back and she closed the door. "I was about to have a glass of wine. Would you like to share one with me?" she invited.

"Yes, I'd like to."

Her gaze roamed the length of him, and she thought, yes, she *would like to* as well, but the thought had nothing to do with a glass of wine. Had those gorgeous green eyes darkened just a bit?

She moved away from the door to stroll toward the kitchen and he walked beside her. Out of the corner of her eye she watched him taking note of the changes she'd made. Flowers, new pictures on the walls and pretty curtains to replace the boring blinds. Going shopping with his mom and sisters-in-law on Saturday had been great. They had taken her to stores that kept her within her budget.

Sloan could just imagine what he was thinking. She'd been busy and she hoped he assumed she'd been much too occupied to even remember he existed. Maybe she wouldn't go that far, but she hoped he hadn't thought she'd missed him, even if she had.

When they reached the kitchen, he stopped in the doorway, probably noticing the changes in here, as well. She placed the gift he'd given her on the table before going straight to the wine bottle on the counter. Opening a cabinet, she pulled out two glasses.

"Need help with anything?" he asked.

"No, I've got this," she said, and a part of her wished she had him, too. She blamed her thoughts on his sisters-in-law. It was obvious they loved being married to their

Steele husbands. It didn't take long to discover they also enjoyed bedtime with their spouses. Could sex be that exciting and enjoyable? Evidently for them it was, which made her wonder if she had made a mistake allowing Carlos to be her first and last. Was there something she'd been missing? Listening to them had given her the impression that maybe she had.

"The place looks nice," he said. "I like all the changes you've made."

"Thanks," she said, looking at him quickly before returning her attention to pouring the wine.

"You look nice, too, Sloan."

She glanced down at herself. He had to be kidding. She was in pj's and fairly decent. She wasn't wearing a bra, but she doubted he would notice.

It was only when she carried the glasses of wine over to the table that he moved away from the doorway to join her. "Thanks."

Deciding to get her mind onto something else and off him, she asked, "Have you gotten the payment information for the car yet?"

"No."

She nodded. "What about the printout for the payment plan information for the loan? Or the papers on the apartment here?"

"No and no. There's no rush."

There was for her. "I need to be able to figure all that into my budget. I bought one of those online programs to help me keep things straight." When she sat down, he eased into the chair across from her. Before taking a sip of her wine, she decided to open his gift. "Oh, Mercury. It's beautiful." He'd given her a crystal paperweight in the shape of a globe.

"I heard the good news about your job with Miss Universe. Congratulations. I understand you'll be traveling a lot internationally. I thought that globe would be a reminder that all the world is out there for you to see."

Yes, it was, and she wished she could say she was ready for the adventure, but she wasn't. She still had to uncover things regarding her parents. Namely why it was so important to them that she marry Harold. "I have a place on my desk for it."

"Good."

Placing the gift aside, she then took a couple of sips of her wine. She tried not looking at him, but couldn't help it. When she did, she discovered he'd been looking at her. She swallowed. "Eli called right before you arrived."

"Did he hear from your grandfather's attorney?"

"Yes, and Eli's coming here in the morning to discuss it."

"I see."

Did he expect her to ask him to join her when his brother dropped by tomorrow? He had avoided her for the past few days. She assumed that was his way of letting her know that not only did she need to find a permanent solution to her problem, but that she needed to do it without him.

"Sloan?"

She glanced over at him. "Yes."

"I owe you an explanation."

She couldn't imagine what kind of explanation he thought he owed her. Hadn't he told her she needed to find a solution to her problem? Then what did she do? She used him as a temporary fix. "No, you don't."

"I honestly believe that I do."

He looked troubled by something. She hadn't picked up on it when he first arrived, but now she did. Maybe the wine had loosened him up a bit; she wasn't sure. Then it dawned on her that whatever was bothering him involved her. Why?

"Okay, if you feel that way, then what's your explanation?"

He'd been looking at her, holding her gaze in a way that made her more aware of him than ever before. When he didn't say anything but continued to stare at her, her heart raced. His look was affecting her.

Clearing her throat, she said, "So, what's this about, Mercury?"

He broke eye contact with her for a quick second. Then he met her gaze again and said, "The reason I put distance between us is because I was tempted to do something that I didn't think you were ready for."

She lifted a brow. "What?"

"To be seduced by a Steele. More specifically, to be seduced by this Steele."

There, he'd said it. He'd told her the root of his problem. However, from the look on her face he had a feeling she didn't fully understand. Did she need him to break it down further? Did he need to tell her how he went to bed dreaming of making love to her? How just sitting across from her at this table was nearly driving him insane?

From the time she'd opened her front door, his attention had been drawn to the nipples poking against the fabric of her top. His mouth had watered immediately at the thought of sliding one or both into his mouth with good, hard sucks. Then he would...

"Obviously you think seducing me is something I'd have no say about, Mercury."

A beguiling smile tugged at his lips. "The only thing you'd be saying is *Please move to the next level*, Sloan. When it comes to seduction, I'm an expert," he added.

There was no need to go into detail about how he typically didn't have to seduce women because they were often trying to seduce him. When he walked into a room, he recognized the predatory gazes, which always made things easy for him.

"So, that's where you've been? Putting your seduction skills to work," she said in a lighthearted tone.

He'd seen a flash of something in her eyes that gave him pause. Hurt. Something twisted his gut. Was that what she thought? That over the past four days he'd been holding a sex-a-thon? And why did it matter if she did think it? It wouldn't have been the first time, if he'd had one. He was single and didn't owe anyone an explanation or an apology for what he did. It was nobody's business. Definitely not hers.

Then why was unexpected guilt still twisting his gut? And why did he feel it was imperative that she know he hadn't been with a woman? That whether he liked it or not, for some reason, she was the only woman he wanted.

In his arms. In his bed. In his life…

That last thought nearly knocked him out of his chair because he didn't do the life thing. He did the sex thing with women. Why would she be any different?

Because Sloan *was* different.

He knew they were attracted to each other; that had been obvious. However, they'd managed to control things and there was no doubt they would have continued to do so… At least she would have. Temptation would have overtaken him if they'd spent more time together.

"Sorry to disappoint you, but I've been busy the last four days doing things that didn't involve women," he said. "I've been handling clients. A few hiccups came up with several players that I had to take care of."

He took a sip of his wine and watched her. Did she know his words had placed a quick smile on her lips that he probably wasn't supposed to have seen? That pretty much let him know she wasn't disappointed that his last four days had been boring.

She wasn't saying anything and then it dawned on him that she was looking at him, not with a predatory gaze but a curious one. And she'd zeroed in on his mouth. He glanced at her chest. The budded tips of her nipples were pressing even more against the fabric of her top. He couldn't help his lusty smile that shifted back to her eyes.

"I think I have a problem where you are concerned, Sloan."

She licked her lips and it was as if he could feel her doing so. "Do you?"

"Yes."

He refused to tell her anything different, not when he could clearly read desire in her eyes. Did she not know what seeing it was doing to him? That was why he'd felt it was best to stay away. Not just because she was getting to him, but because he was letting her. She was tempting him into breaking one very important rule: never let a woman get to him again.

"You know what you told me, Mercury. When you have a problem it's up to you to find a solution."

"I thought I had, which was why I stayed away," he said, not trying to mask the frustration in his voice. He then grazed his fingers across her hand and watched as her nipples got even harder. Something hot, passionate and wild moved between them. Something he wasn't sure either of them could stop.

"You might not like the solution I come up with, Sloan."

"Try me."

He lifted a brow. Had she just told him to try her? In that case...

He slowly stood from the table and came around to where she sat. He extended his hand to her, she took it, and he gently tugged her from the chair. He then eased closer to her, deliberately brushing their bodies, certain she felt the evidence of his desire for her when he did so.

She didn't know it, but being seduced by this Steele was a three-step process. TLC. Tempt. Lure. Conquer.

"Say it again, Sloan." He wanted to make sure she understood what she was saying. He had a feeling that, in the end, she wouldn't be his conquest; he would become hers. The thought of that didn't bother him.

"I said, try me, Mercury."

He still needed to make sure because there was no going back. "Do you know what trying you entails?" Maybe he needed to let her know that trying her meant doing it the Mercury Steele way.

"Yes, I know."

She thought she knew, but he definitely had a few surprises for her... He knew his expression had instantly become predatory, wolfish and seductive. He then wrapped his arms around her waist. First up was tempting her. Giving her a sampling of what to expect.

More than ready to get his plan of seduction started, he leaned in and slanted his mouth over hers, knowing this time it wouldn't stop with a kiss.

Eighteen

Sloan fought back a moan. What in the world was Mercury doing to her? Kissing her this way? Raw and possessive. They had kissed before, several times, but she'd always managed to keep up with him. Now he was leaving her far behind. But that wasn't all he was doing.

How had his body seemed to sink deeper into her when they were standing up and still fully clothed? Yet she felt the hardness of his erection pressing against her, scoping out the best spot for entry. Since there was only one possibility, she figured it was his way of trying to drive her mad. And it was working.

Never had any man taken this much time with her. No rush job like Carlos. Mercury was taking his time driving her wild with desire. It was a degree of desire she hadn't known she was capable of feeling. She was so wrapped up in their kiss that she hadn't known he'd opened the buttons to the front of her top until she felt the air hit her chest. How had he managed that when their bodies were pressed together?

And then he was finally releasing her mouth and taking a step back. She opened her eyes to find him studying her breasts like they were a piece of art. When he used the pad of his thumb to caress a nipple, she could actually feel heat flowing between her legs. Did he have any idea what he was doing to her?

Her breasts were sensitive and one of the erotic points in her body. She'd tried to get Carlos to pamper them, and he refused, saying he was a between-the-legs man. That was when she'd decided to make him one and done. But Mercury was indulging her breasts as if he'd known how much pleasure she would get from him doing so. And she *was* getting pleasure.

"You like that, Sloan?"

Unable to speak when his thumb moved to the other breast, she merely nodded her head.

"I knew you would."

How had he known? As if she'd spoken that question out loud, he said, "A man intent on pleasuring a woman makes it his business to know what turns her on. By the time I'm finished with you, I will know every erogenous zone on your body." And with that said, he leaned in and sucked a nipple into his mouth.

Sloan fought back a scream when his tongue hungrily lapped her nipple. If he only knew how he was making her feel. Maybe he did know. He'd pretty much said he was an expert when it came to seducing a woman, and it seemed he hadn't been lying.

No longer able to fight back a scream, she let it rip.

Sensations tore through her, more powerful than any dreams she'd had. Never in her wildest dream could she have imagined this. Never.

Before she could recover, Mercury had left her breasts and was kneeling in front of her. Through dazed eyes she saw him jerk down her shorts. Was he shocked to discover she wasn't wearing any panties? She didn't have time to wonder because that was when he used his hands to widen her legs. The next thing she knew, his mouth and tongue had invaded her.

Heaven help her.

Was he trying to kill her? His tongue pushed inside her, then licked her like she was his favorite treat. She grabbed his head to push him away, and then when sensations began rippling through her, she tightened her hold and moved her hips back and forth against his mouth. The more she did, the greedier he became. Was she telling him in a chant not to stop?

Another orgasm tore into her and she screamed again. Her body trembled inside and out and she still held firm to him, tossing her head back and sucking in air. It was only when the last spasm had left her body that he eased back up to his feet and kissed her, letting her taste herself on his tongue. How scandalous.

He released her mouth and she opened her eyes. The look in his almost had her coming again. Never had she seen so much desire as she did in his green depths. "Sloan?"

It seemed as if he'd breathed out her name. "Yes?" she said, barely getting out the single word.

"I've just tempted you. Do you know what's next?"

He'd done more than tempted her. He had to know

that. She'd never known temptation to be anything like this. "No, I don't know what's next."

"Lure. I want to lure you to your bedroom to finish what we've started. My plan of seduction is a three-part process. TLC. Tempt, lure and conquer. Now to lure you."

She watched as he crooked his finger and began walking backward. Not caring that she was naked and he wasn't, she slowly followed him, going where he lured and knowing what he had in store when she got there would be worth it.

Mercury was convinced that never had luring a woman to her own bedroom been so freaking awesome. He was walking backward, so it was a good thing he remembered the layout of her place. Sloan was holding his mind hostage.

There was just something about a naked woman following you with a look in her eyes that all but said, *I can't wait.*

Neither could he, especially while allowing his gaze to roam all over her, from head to toe. She had a beautiful body with curves in all the right places. Her breasts were perfectly formed and the area between her legs was a gift from heaven. Not for the first time he thought she had that refined walk that mothers were sending their daughters to Brittany's etiquette school to perfect.

When they finally reached her bedroom, he glanced around, noticing the changes in here as well and the dominant color. Blue, blue and more blue. He smiled. However, the decor of the room wasn't what was on his mind.

He wanted to get a naked Sloan in her bed and join her there.

"We're here," he said, slowly walking over to her. "I lured you into your own bedroom."

"Conquer is next, right?" she asked when he came to a stop in front of her. He could see the pulse rapidly beating in her neck and he felt her anticipation. He liked that.

She had no qualms about what they were about to do. Neither did he.

"Yes," he said, sliding his hand between her legs and loving the fact that she was still wet. "Do you know what that entails?"

"No. Tell me."

He had no problem doing that. "Now I want to make you come while I'm inside you."

He watched her features when his fingers eased inside her. She was so hot and the expression on her face was just as heated.

"You have your clothes on," she said, like she was just realizing that fact.

"Not for long." He then stared at her and realized just what she'd come to mean to him over the past few days. More than he'd wanted. More than he was ready to admit.

"You're ready for my final part of seduction? Conquering?" he asked her.

"Yes."

"Good. I'm about to give you all the pleasure any one woman can handle." While saying those words he moved closer so his body could brush against her naked one. Specifically, he wanted her to feel just how hard his erection was for her. "It wants you, Sloan."

"And I want it, Mercury."

He smiled. Then, sweeping her up into his arms, he moved toward the bed.

When Mercury placed her in the middle of the mattress, he leaned in and placed a finger at her chin to lift her gaze to his. Sloan's heart beat hard at the look she saw in the depths of his green eyes.

"You have no idea how much I've thought of you these last four days, Sloan. How hard I've been fighting my need for you or how many nights I've gone to bed dreaming of being inside you. At this moment I need you with every breath flowing through my lungs."

His words, spoken so seductively, caused every part of Sloan to come alive, to want him as much as he'd just said he wanted her. No man had ever expressed a need for her the way he'd just done. Then he released her chin and moved away from the bed and she watched. She knew what they were about to share would be one of those incredible experiences that she would remember forever.

She pulled herself into a better position to watch what he was doing, not wanting to miss a thing. Her gaze followed Mercury's fingers as they went to the buttons of his shirt. As he eased each button free, she saw his chest and the curly hair covering it. She tried hard not to moan in total admiration at the sight but found it impossible.

He looked at her when he tossed his shirt aside. "You okay, Sloan?"

How could he ask her that while standing there shirtless with a body that could make a woman drool? "I think so."

"Well, I hope so. Are you changing your mind about anything?"

Changing her mind wouldn't be happening. "You don't have to worry about that, Mercury."

He smiled as his fingers went to the zipper of his pants. She couldn't help it when her breath caught. It seemed every nerve ending within her came alive as he slowly dragged down his zipper and then proceeded to ease down his pants and black briefs over a pair of powerfully built thighs.

She'd never seen a naked man before. Carlos didn't count since he'd undressed in the dark. But now she saw Mercury and knew without a doubt he was beautifully made. Seeing him in the flesh had her in a sensual daze. She lowered her gaze to his middle and shivered all over. He was big. Real big. Extra, extra big.

"It will be okay, Sloan," he said, then proceeded to sheathe himself with a condom.

She moved her gaze to his eyes. She hoped so. Had he seen the distress in her face? When he strolled back toward her she didn't have time to think any more about what he might or might not have seen. No man should have such a sexy walk.

Placing a knee on the bed, he whispered her name and then reached down and drew her naked body to his, connecting their mouths. The moment his tongue slid inside her mouth she knew what to do. She hungrily latched on to it, following his lead and returning the kiss with the same intensity he was using. The feel and scent of him were drugging her mind.

She felt him lowering her to the bed cushions without dislodging their mouths, and she experienced the moment he positioned his body over hers. Then she felt his erection right at her opening. He released her mouth to look down at her, locking their gazes together as he slowly began easing inside her. Instinctively, she wrapped her legs around him. Drawing in a sharp breath, she felt a quick moment of pain. Then he thrust into her. She drew in a deep breath, feeling him deeply.

"You okay?"

She tightened her arms around his neck. "Not sure I could ever be better."

Her response pleased him if that smile was anything to go by. Then he began moving, slow at first, as all kinds of delicious sensations overtook her. He established a rhythm for them, one she thought was destined to drive her mad with desire.

Just like with his kisses, she began following his lead. She moved her body in sync with his, arching her hips and grinding her thighs. Each one of his thrusts seemed to ignite even more passion within her, and when he increased the pace of the strokes, she broke eye contact with him to toss her head back and forth and from side to side.

He leaned in and whispered naughty words in her ear. Her entire body shuddered when he described in intimate detail what they would do all night. Then his thrusts became even more powerful, going even deeper, and she became lost in the pleasure.

Over and over again he pushed her to the edge, and before she could fall, he would whip her back again. Why was he torturing her this way? She called out his name in protest, and that was when he whispered in a husky tone, "Let's come together, baby. Always together."

His words seemed to trigger something inside her. She screamed his name at the same exact moment he hollered hers. He threw his head back. His thrusts kept coming and she kept taking them, loving the way her body exploded under his.

At that moment she knew she had fallen in love with Mercury. It didn't matter if he loved her back or if this was only a seduction by a Steele.

It only mattered that she loved him.

Nineteen

When Mercury opened his eyes, it took him a moment to remember where he was. Definitely not in his own bed with all this frilly, lacy stuff covering the bed with curtains to match. At least he approved of the color blue.

He then glanced down at the woman in his arms. He smiled, loving the feel of the warm body tucked beside him, with his legs thrown over hers. Sloan was still sleeping, which wasn't surprising, considering all they'd done through the night. His goal had been to give her all the pleasure she could handle, and it seemed she'd been able to handle a lot. He'd figured she would tire out, but she'd been determined to keep up with him. His Sloan had discovered that, when it came to sex, he had endless energy. He wholly appreciated her efforts.

His Sloan?

He closed his eyes, not wanting to think of her or any woman as his. Needing to push the thought from his mind, his gaze scanned the room. He liked her decorating ideas. She'd been busy this weekend. She probably hadn't thought of him at all, but he had thought about her. He hadn't known a woman he'd met less than a week ago could have such an impact on him. But she had.

His gaze returned to her. She looked beautiful while she slept, but then, she looked beautiful while being made love to, as well. More than once he had watched her come, and the way her features contorted in pleasure filled him with so much enjoyment.

Glancing at the clock on her nightstand, he saw it was close to eight in the morning. It had not been his intention to spend the night, but things had turned out that way. He had no complaints.

"Good morning, Mercury."

Her sleepy-eyed smile was beautiful. *She* was beautiful. He thought about how they'd met and everything that had transpired since. The woman had entered his world on a series of misadventures. But he would gladly experience them all again if he could be assured that he would have another night like the one he'd shared last night with her.

"Good morning. Are you okay?" He knew he'd asked her that a lot, but her well-being meant everything to him. She pulled herself up, fully stretching, seemingly not at all bothered by her nakedness. If it didn't bother her, it certainly didn't bother him. In fact, he liked looking at her sexy body.

"Yes, I'm wonderful. You were wonderful, Mercury."

He'd heard that before from other women, but hearing it from her meant a hell of a lot. "Thanks, and you were wonderful, too."

"You're just being kind because I didn't know what I was doing most of the time. I was basically following your lead."

And she'd done a good job of it. "Trust me—you were wonderful."

His words brought an even brighter smile to her lips. "And just to think last night was the first time I've ever had an orgasm."

He blinked. "Excuse me?"

"I said I never experienced an orgasm before last night. Couldn't you tell?"

No, he couldn't, considering she'd had her first one with him while his mouth had been on her breasts while in her kitchen. "Are you saying Cunningham dropped the ball? No pun intended."

She laughed. "None taken since Harold and I never shared a bed. I would suggest it, thinking it would be the thing to do since we were engaged, but he wasn't interested. Of course, I eventually discovered why. He was into a relationship with someone else. At least he wasn't trying to sleep with the both of us. Some men would have, you know."

His mind was reeling at what she'd just said. "You weren't a virgin last night, right?"

Hell, he hoped not. He'd never wanted to be any woman's first, thanks to his mother's lectures and her psychological analysis of what that meant for a woman. According to the Principles of Eden, a woman never forgot her first guy. She would remember him forever.

He hadn't wanted to be remembered by any woman that long.

"Virgin? Heck no. I had sex with Carlos in college once. It was awful."

He nodded. "Carlos was your boyfriend?"

"Yes, at the time. For me it was one and done." She broke eye contact with him to glance over at the clock. "And speaking of time, I need to get up and get dressed. Eli is dropping by at nine. I have extra toiletries under the vanity in that bathroom."

Did she want him to leave? There was only one way to find out. "Will this be a private meeting between you and Eli?"

She glanced back at him. "No. You're welcome to stay if you want. Like I told Harold that night, you already know most of my business anyway. I'm surprised Eli didn't mention anything to you."

Was she kidding? Sloan evidently didn't know how Eli functioned as an attorney. His brother operated on a strict code of ethics. When she'd hired Eli, his by-the-book brother wouldn't share any details of his findings without her permission. "He didn't, but that's fine as long as you don't have a problem with me being here."

She leaned up and wrapped her arms around him. "I don't have a problem with you being here, Mercury."

"Glad to hear it." He then leaned in and captured her mouth with his.

Eli stared hard at his brother when Mercury opened the door to let him into Sloan's apartment. "Why aren't I surprised to find you here?"

Mercury smiled. "I don't know. Why aren't you?"

Before Eli could give a smart-ass answer to Mercury's

smart-ass question, Sloan came out of the kitchen, smiling. "Good morning, Eli. I just made a pot of coffee. Would you like a cup?"

He smiled over at Sloan. "No, thanks. I had a cup earlier. I'd like to go into my report since I have another appointment in a couple of hours."

"Okay," Sloan said, easing down on the sofa with Mercury sitting beside her. "What did Mr. Rivers have to say?"

Eli slid down in the wingback chair opposite of them. "To protect you, the terms of your grandfather's will stated that you will get the proceeds from your trust fund at thirty…unless you marry before then. Then you get it the day after you marry, to do with as you wish."

Sloan's eyes widened in surprise. She hadn't known. "So, Harold was right. My parents are banking on our marriage not only to combine the family's wealth, but for me to bring a dowry."

"Yes, it looks that way," Eli said, standing. "If you need me to do anything else, let me know. I like Charles Rivers. It's obvious he intends to handle business the way your grandfather wanted him to do."

"Thanks, Eli," she said, walking him to the door.

When she returned to the living room, Mercury was standing in the middle of the floor. "Come here," he said, opening his arms to her.

She walked into them, needing a hug and grateful he was there to give her one. He tightened his hold on her and she snuggled closer to him. They'd made love again this morning and then they'd showered together. What she'd told him was true. He was a fantastic lover and had made her feel things she'd never felt before. Things she hadn't thought she'd been capable of feeling.

"Go out of town with me tomorrow."

She leaned back to look up at him. "You want me to go out of town with you?"

"Yes. I'm flying to Dallas for a few days to meet with a potential client. I think getting away will do you good."

She didn't want to think about just how good it would be with him. Another thing she didn't want to think about was how she felt for Mercury.

She loved him.

Drawing in a deep breath, she accepted that, love or no love, a serious relationship was the last thing she needed. She was starting a new life and a new job. She needed time for herself without being crowded by emotions for someone else. But she knew loving Mercury wasn't anything she could put on a shelf to take down when it was convenient.

And she knew that, although she loved Mercury, he didn't love her. Hadn't he told her more than once that he could never love a woman? She had no reason not to take him at his word.

Even so, the thought of spending a couple of days with him sounded nice.

"Sloan?"

She smiled. "I'd love to go to Dallas with you."

Twenty

Mercury sat at his desk steepling his fingers while studying the beautiful view of the mountains outside his office window. Had it been two weeks since he'd persuaded Sloan to go out of town with him? Two whole weeks? He still thought about just how wonderful their trip to Dallas had been and how his life with her had changed since then.

He had never invited a woman anywhere with him and had surprised himself by asking her. But once the shock had worn off, he'd looked forward to spending time with her. When it came to meeting people and putting them at ease, she'd been a natural. He was convinced Brock Dennison's parents would not have entertained signing their son with Mercury if it hadn't been for Sloan. The Dennisons were farmers, and not used to urban ways of life. Because she'd spent so much time with her grandfather on his farm in Texas, Sloan had been able to relate and put the Dennisons at ease. They had loved her.

And he loved her.

That admission had Mercury's heart pounding hard in his chest. He closed his eyes, knowing he'd never expected to admit to feeling those emotions toward any woman ever again, yet here he was, admitting to loving a woman he'd known less than a month.

At that moment she was a woman he couldn't imagine living without.

That was the reason why, since returning to Phoenix, he'd done everything to make her an intricate part of his life. He'd decided to do something he'd never done before, which was to court a woman. He'd taken her to dinner, to the movies, and he'd even shown up at church last Sunday, much to his mother's shock and delight. And he never assumed he had a right to spend the night. He asked or she would ask. Well, she never really asked, since now she was the one using his TLC approach and seducing him with such finesse that he got a hard-on thinking about how she'd go about it.

Unlike the other women in his past, with Sloan it had never been about just a physical attraction. It had been more. Spending time together was what they needed to do to get to know each other better. She'd talked about her grandfather and he could feel the love in her words. He'd also discovered that trust was important to her and it hurt her to find out about her parents' deception. More than once, he'd been tempted to tell her about the car and the apartment and how his name was on both. But he hadn't wanted anything to ruin their time together.

He looked at the packet Pauline had given him this morning, the one that had arrived while he was out on Friday. Namely the payment plan for the loan from his accountant, the paperwork for the car and the lease agreement for her apartment. The time had finally come. He would deliver the packet to her this evening and tell her everything then.

When the buzzer on his intercom went off, he pressed the button. "Yes, Pauline?"

"A Ms. Beverly McClain is on the line for you."

Beverly was the one-night stand that never was. They'd met on a flight to Florida eight years ago, and when they discovered they would be staying at the same hotel, they had agreed to hook up. He hadn't known her divorce from her husband had become final that day, and instead of burning the sheets, he had taken her to dinner, where she'd cried while telling him what an asshole she'd been married to for three years. The next morning they'd met up again for coffee and decided they could be friends, and for the last eight years, they had.

Since then, she'd remarried a great guy who'd made her happy and they had two kids. Beverly worked for the government as one of the heads of Homeland Security. If she was calling him, that meant…

"Please put her through."

When he heard the click, he said, "Beverly?"

"Hello, Mercury. How have you been?"

He smiled. "Great, and you?"

"Pregnant again. You know what that means. Morning sickness is kicking my butt, but I'll survive."

"Of course you will. You always do."

"The reason I was calling was to let you know of activity with the names you gave me. A plane carrying Carter Haywood Donahue landed in Phoenix less than an hour ago. He didn't have any checked luggage."

Mercury nodded. That meant the man didn't intend to stay in Phoenix long. "Thanks. I appreciate the information."

Moments later Mercury stood and reached for his cell phone to let Sloan know her father was in town. Chances were, he'd found out where she lived and would go straight to her place. He quickly changed his mind about phoning Sloan. There was no way he would let her face her tyrant of a father alone.

He had stood and was reaching for his jacket when the buzzer on his desk sounded. "Yes, Pauline?"

"Quade Westmoreland is on line two."

"Thanks."

Sitting back down in his chair, Mercury said, "Quade? You have something for me?"

"Yes, man, I do."

Sloan ended her conference call with the pageant committee feeling excited about what they'd told her. She had two more weeks to enjoy life as she now knew it before her work with them officially began. She had been assigned five countries. All five were now holding their individual pageants that would determine the woman to represent their country in the Miss Universe pageant in December.

She leaned back in her chair and thought about her five days in Dallas with Mercury and the time they'd constantly been together since. More often than not, he would spend the night after taking her to dinner or to the movies or just hanging out at her place watching television. And she'd been invited to his place more

than once to spend the night. He'd told her that he'd
never invited a woman overnight before.

More than once she wondered if there had been a
reason for him telling her that. Had he been insinuat-
ing that she was special in some way? That he could
possibly love her as much as she loved him? He'd even
invited her to attend his parents' Thursday dinners and
she felt right at home. No one had questioned their relationship. It was as if his family was giving them the
time they needed to build the relationship they wanted.
At least the one she wanted.

Did he?

Mercury saw to her every need, both in and out
of the bedroom. She was feeling like a woman who
was living the independent life she'd always wanted.
She had to answer to no one. And she was involved
with a man who understood how much her feelings of
self-worth and her happiness mattered. She was free
of dependency and she felt like a new person. A person in love.

She wanted to believe the last two weeks were the
beginning of something special between her and Mercury. She wanted to believe the more they got to know
each other the stronger their relationship would grow.

She wanted to believe she could have both her independence and Mercury, too, because he understood
how much not depending on anyone meant to her. He
respected her desire for liberation.

A smile touched her lips when she remembered how
he'd even helped by allowing her to test her dominance
in bed. She'd loved it. He'd loved it. She had a lot to
learn and he'd happily volunteered to teach her.

She heard the sound of the doorbell. It wasn't even

noon yet. Who would be visiting her? Mercury had said he would be going into the office this morning to get caught up on work. She then remembered that she had ordered a few things from an online office-supply store and figured the delivery was being made.

Going to the door, she looked out the peephole and her breath caught. She felt like someone had kicked her in the gut. It was her father. What was he doing here? It didn't matter because he was here.

For the first time in her life she would not let him intimidate her. Thanks to Mercury, she was more self-assured than ever and wouldn't let her father treat her like less than the adult she was.

Opening the door, she faced the man she loved but who for years never knew how to show or return that love. "Dad, come in."

He didn't say hello. He just walked past her like the thought of even being here agitated him. When she closed the door and turned, she saw him glancing around her apartment with disdain.

"Dad, what are you doing here?" There was no reason to ask how he'd found her. He kept one of the best detective agencies in Ohio on retainer.

His scornful gaze switched to her. "I am here to take you home, Sloan Elizabeth. I expected Harold to be man enough to handle you, but it seems you're being difficult."

At any other time, his harsh reprimand would have brought her back in check, would definitely have made her lower her head in shame, but not this time. Carter H. Donahue was going to discover that his child who had been a disappointment was more like him in some ways than a son could ever be. The one thing she had inherited from him was his stubbornness.

"News flash, Dad. I am not going anywhere with you. Did you not listen to what I told you when I left Cincinnati? What I'm sure Harold told you I said when he returned to report back to you? Harold and I aren't getting married."

He rolled his eyes. "Of course the two of you can't get married in June now. That's not enough time to plan for the huge wedding the two of you deserve," he said irritably. "You'll be happy to know that the Cunninghams, your mother and I have decided that an August wedding for you and Harold will work."

She would be happy to know...? Sloan just stood there and stared at her father. His assumption that he had her unwavering obedience was her fault. In the past he'd given her a mandate and she'd marched to whatever beat he played.

She'd changed.

"Dad, read my lips. I am not marrying Harold. I love my life here and I am not leaving."

There was no way she would tell him about her job with the Miss Universe pageant or else he would ruin that, too. That was why she'd made sure all her employment information was listed under S. E. Donahue.

"So you'd rather be a kept woman than the wife of an honorable man?"

She frowned at her father. "What are you talking about?"

He eased down on her sofa without her having issued an invitation for him to do so. "You think I haven't checked out Mercury Steele and his family?"

Sloan's heart began pounding again and she tried

hard to remember what Mercury had always said. Her father couldn't touch his family. "So, you've checked them out. Then you know they don't scare easily."

"Yes, and under any other circumstances I wouldn't mind doing business with them, but for your future I'm betting my money on the Cunninghams."

Doing business? She wasn't surprised that he saw any marriage for her as a business deal. "You're not the only one who can have people checked out. I know all about my trust fund and the reason you want me and Harold to marry. You think you can get your hands on it."

"Of course I can. I'm your father and will look out for your best interest."

"No, Dad, you are looking out for your own interest. There's no way I'll let you or the Cunninghams touch what Granddad left for me."

His facial features contorted in anger. "So is this how you claim the independence you want so much, by being Mercury Steele's kept woman? Do you think he will make you anything other than his whore? You'd rather be a man's whore than his wife?"

He paused as if he needed a moment to catch his breath before continuing. "Regardless of what you told Harold about Mercury Steele being your fiancé, his reputation proves he's not going to be any woman's husband. If you think he will marry you, then you are a fool. Your mother and I raised you for more than being some man's kept woman."

That was the third time he'd referred to her as being a kept woman. "I have no idea what you are talking about."

Her father's features suddenly changed, and his

mouth actually seemed to twitch in amusement. As if it suddenly occurred to him that he knew something she didn't. "You don't know, do you?"

"I don't know what?"

"That you aren't the independent woman you think you are. You left home because you thought your mother and I were being manipulative and you wanted your freedom and didn't want to be dependent on anyone. Yet you are dependent on Mercury Steele."

She frowned. Evidently that detective agency he retained had found out about the twenty-thousand-dollar loan Mercury had made to her. "So, he loaned me money to help get me on my feet. Big deal. I am paying him back."

"What about that car you're driving and this apartment. Both are in his name."

"They aren't."

"Yes, they are."

Sloan's frown deepened. That wasn't true, but she didn't have the paperwork to prove otherwise because Mercury hadn't given any documents to her.

What if her father's claim *was* true?

She refused to believe it because, of all people, Mercury knew how much she wanted her independence. Why would he keep something like that from her?

"So, what do you have to say to that, Sloan Elizabeth?"

When she didn't reply because she was still reeling, in his authoritative voice he said, "Now do what you're told and go pack. I've reserved a ticket in your name. Our flight leaves for Cincinnati in three hours."

"I hate to disappoint you, Mr. Donahue, but Sloan isn't going anywhere with you."

Sloan jerked around to find Mercury standing by the door. Legs braced apart with his arms folded over his chest, he had a fierce look on his face. How did he get in when she'd locked the door? Then she saw the key in his hand. A key to her apartment that she hadn't given him. At that moment she knew her father had been telling the truth.

Twenty-One

Mercury refused to look at Sloan's father. The man was of no significance, but his daughter was, and Mercury's gaze was trained on her. She meant everything to him and he refused to let anyone, including her father, devalue her or put ideas in her head about her meaning nothing to him.

When he saw the pain in her eyes, he knew his mistake had been in not telling her the truth weeks ago. "It's time you left, Mr. Donahue."

"Oh, I guess you do have the right to put me out since this apartment is leased to you and not to my daughter."

Mercury ignored the man's words. "We need to talk privately," he said to Sloan.

"My daughter has nothing to say to you."

Mercury glanced at the other man. Mercury knew

his gaze reflected the anger he felt. "Sloan can speak for herself." He had a mind to kick the man out, literally, but figured even if he was an ass, he was Sloan's father.

"You're right—she can, and I'm sure she will make the right decision." The older man then moved to Sloan. "I'm going back to the airport and will wait for you. Here's your ticket," he said, placing the ticket on the coffee table. "I expect you to make that plane with me, Sloan Elizabeth."

Carter H. Donahue then walked to the door and slammed it shut behind him.

Mercury couldn't help but stare at the door the man had just walked out of, not believing what he'd witnessed. No wonder Sloan had needed to escape her father's control. The man was worse than a tyrant. He was a damn dictator.

"Is what my father claimed true, Mercury? Do you own my car and is this apartment in your name?"

"Yes," he said, without hesitation, turning back to look at Sloan. "Remember our discussion on temporary fixes? I made decisions to use a couple."

He then came to stand in front of her, but not before tossing the package he carried onto the same coffee table where her father had tossed the plane ticket. "I had planned to explain things to you tonight when I dropped by. If you care to check that packet, you'll see the car and the apartment are both in your name now."

"B-but why?"

He shoved his hands into his pockets. "Because I knew how much both meant to you, and without me handling things the way I did, you would not have gotten either. I wanted to see you happy."

Sloan broke eye contact with him to look at the package. She then looked back at him. "Why didn't you tell me?"

Mercury knew he needed to make her understand. "Because the one thing I had gotten to know about you was that being independent meant everything to you. It boosted your confidence in yourself, and I wanted to help make it happen. Had I told you then, you would have fought me on it. Look how you didn't want the money I gave you to open that bank account. I'm used to women wanting my money more than not wanting it."

She placed her hands on her hips and glared at him. "Then maybe you need to know better women."

"True, and I found that out the hard way—trust me." He moved past her to look out the window at the lake. He then turned to her. "While in college I fell in love with a woman who I thought loved me back. I later found out that all she wanted was to hook up with a football player who she thought had a future in the NFL. Like you, she had parents with goals established for her. They wanted their daughter to marry for money."

She eyed him speculatively. "What happened?"

He drew in a deep breath. "I was injured and was told I would never play football again. That's when I discovered my purpose in her life. She moved on to another player."

Sloan raised a brow. "But you did play again?"

"Yes. I was determined to show her that she'd written me off too soon. It took me an entire year of rehab and therapy, but I came back better and stronger than ever. And I told myself I would never love another woman. All they see are dollar signs. Not one proved me wrong…until I met you. You're the only woman I know who prefers being poor to being rich."

She rolled her eyes. "I wouldn't take it that far, Mercury. I like nice things like anyone else. I just never want money to define me."

"Most women wouldn't care about such a definition."

Spine straight and her chin tilted high, she said, "When are you going to realize I'm not like most women?"

Leaving his spot by the window, he slowly walked over to stand in front of her. "I realized it the moment I accepted that I had fallen in love with you."

She released a shocked gasp. "You love me?"

He nodded. "Yes, I love you," he said, thinking the shocked look on her face was so painfully beautiful. At that moment nothing mattered more than for her to believe what he was saying. "I absolutely, positively, undeniably, unequivocally love you, Sloan."

She didn't say anything, but he saw the lone tear that fell from her eye. "You love me even knowing what kind of parents I have?" she asked in a voice filled with emotion.

He drew her into his arms. "Your parents have nothing to do with you other than that they created you. I just hope you're not going to rush off to the airport and leave town with your father. I couldn't handle it if you left me."

"Oh, Mercury," she said, leaning up on tiptoe to brush a kiss across his lips. He was about to slant his mouth over hers when she said, "And just so you know, I already love you. I love you so much, Mercury."

Surprise lit his eyes and he smiled before taking her lips in an open-mouth kiss that seemed to last forever. When he finally released her mouth, she buried her face against his neck.

Mercury closed his eyes and inhaled her scent. He was thankful for the misadventures that had brought her into his life. However, there was something he had to tell her. Something she needed to know that Quade had found out.

Lifting her off her feet, he held her securely in his arms, carried her over to the sofa and sat down with her in his lap. "There is something I need to tell you. It's about your father."

She lifted a brow. "What?"

"I told you that my cousin Quade, who used to work for the CIA, was investigating your father for me."

"Yes, you told me that."

"Well, Quade called me right before I came over here."

She nodded. "And?"

"Your father is being blackmailed. That's why he needs money. He's borrowed as much as he could get and now you're the only source he has left. Namely your trust fund. That's why he needs you to marry Cunningham."

"Why is he being blackmailed? What has he done?"

Mercury paused and then said, "A couple of years ago, he and a couple more bankers took what was supposedly a business trip to this island off the Caribbean. The entire weekend they were sexually involved with underage girls who'd been kidnapped to pleasure them. Some as young as eleven."

Sloan's hand flew to her mouth. "No!"

"Yes. What these businessmen didn't know was that cameras had been installed in the bedrooms to deliberately blackmail them later. All the businessmen who participated in the orgy have received calls demanding money in exchange for the blackmailers' silence."

Anger flared in Sloan's eyes. "How could any of those men have participated in such a thing?" She then said, "If your cousin found out about it, that means..."

"Yes, the FBI is on it, and it's just a matter of time before arrests are made. That will include your father and I just wanted you to be prepared." He paused again. "And I wanted you to know I will be here for you. In fact, all the Steeles will be. My family loves you as much as I do."

"Oh, Mercury." He saw tears shimmering in her eyes. In the future he would put more smiles than tears in her eyes.

He then leaned in and captured her mouth again before standing with her in his arms and heading for the bedroom.

At twenty-five Sloan finally knew how it felt to be loved by a man. To be totally cherished. And when Mercury placed her on the bed and stood back and stared at her, she knew how it felt to be desired.

She didn't have to sense his need for her. She saw blatant evidence of it. Then there was the look in his eyes that held so many sexual promises. She knew she was in for a wild ride. And a very satisfying one at that.

"What are you thinking about, sweetheart?" he asked her.

She couldn't help but smile. "I'm thinking about

how much I love you. How grateful I am for having you in my life and how I'd give anything if you stayed."

A serious expression appeared in his features. "I'm not going anywhere. Neither are you. We're stuck in this crazy thing called love together."

Yes, they were stuck in it together.

She reclined into a comfortable position and watched as he began removing his clothes. She always enjoyed this part, which left her wondering how any man could be so well toned, so powerfully built and so masterfully sexy. She wished she could concentrate on other things, but when he removed his clothes, his body always had her full attention. And when he finally stood in front of her, splendidly naked, she couldn't help but be in awe of his masculine beauty.

"Now for your clothes," he said, drawing her attention to his mouth. It was a mouth she totally enjoyed kissing. Over the past weeks, he had shown her how to kiss him in so many enjoyable ways. He was right; she wasn't going anywhere. She honestly pitied her father if he truly believed she would be showing up at the airport to return to Cincinnati with him. That wouldn't be happening.

She watched Mercury move to the bed and she leaned toward him. He always took his time undressing her, removing every piece of her clothing, then meticulously touching the areas he uncovered. He enjoyed fulfilling all her sexual needs. Making up for lost time and making sure she got everything she wanted and then some.

She drew in a deep breath when his hand slid beneath her T-shirt, felt the braless breasts and unerringly went to her nipples. The moment his fingers touched them, she felt a tingling sensation between her legs. "Mercury…"

"Tell me what you want, baby."

He'd first asked her that on their trip to Dallas and she'd had a bucket list. But not tonight. More than anything, she needed the feel of him buried deep inside her. The feel of him claiming her as his and her making him hers. That was what she both wanted and needed.

"I need you inside me. Now," she said in a desperate tone before leaning in to nip at his jaw.

He must have heard the urgency in her voice because he suddenly ripped her T-shirt over her head and then grabbed the waistband of her shorts. In one lightning-quick motion, he removed both the shorts and her panties. Reaching out, he swiftly positioned her body against the mass of pillows, bedcovers and cushions and immediately joined her there, straddling her.

He captured her wrists in his hands, held them over her head and looked down into her eyes. "If my lady doesn't want seduction this time, I have no problem bypassing that part."

Sloan smiled. She had been seduced by this Steele more times than she could count. This time she wanted to go straight to being conquered. "Take me, Mercury. Make me yours."

The gaze staring down at her was fiercely possessive when he said, "You're already mine, Sloan."

And then she felt the full length of the huge, solid erection slide into her. In response, her inner muscles tightened around him, holding him and squeezing him. She knew he'd felt it when a satisfying grin covered his features. "I love it when your body tries holding me hostage like that."

She smiled up at him. "Just getting all I can." He had stopped using a condom the last time he'd made love to her, after establishing the fact that they were both healthy and she'd been on the pill for some time.

"And I plan to give you all you want."

Then he began moving, just the way she liked and, more important, the way she needed. The feel of his shaft stroking inside her had her moaning his name over and over again. He released her hands to grab hold of her hips, lifting her up to assure she received every one of his hard thrusts. Their bodies were so in tune. She closed her eyes as he began pushing even deeper inside her, setting a rhythm and giving her everything she craved.

His male scent filled her nostrils, stimulating her senses. When his thrusts grew harder and harder, she moaned more than just his name. She said words she'd heard him say while climaxing with her. Naughty words. Erotic words. Words she hadn't known existed until he'd said them. Words she now found so wickedly sexy.

"Do I need to start washing your mouth out with soap?" he asked her, leaning close to her ear and not missing a beat with his steady stream of thrusts.

"Not with soap, but I can think of something else," she told him, remembering how just last week he'd taught her to please him with her mouth. He said she was too good a student and would be the death of him yet.

When he threw his head back and hollered her name, his actions triggered an orgasm of gigantic proportions. In that instant she wasn't sure what was the loudest. His holler or her scream. It didn't matter. Nothing mattered but this and each other.

She knew at that moment that Mercury Morris Steele was all she wanted and needed in her life.

"Will you marry me, Sloan?"

She opened her eyes to stare up into his. She felt his shaft stretching her again. "Marry you?"

"Yes."

What man could ask a woman that in the middle of making love? She smiled. Mercury could. Mercury would. Mercury just did. Her answer would be just as spontaneous as his question had been. "Yes! I will marry you."

He smiled down at her before capturing her mouth with a long, deep, thorough kiss. And then he began moving again, putting her inner muscles to work once more. Both of them were determined to drive each other off the edge. They had tonight and the rest of their lives to make it happen. And they would.

Epilogue

One month later

Mercury smiled when he entered his condo to the aroma of food. Since finishing her cooking class, Sloan enjoyed coming over to his place and surprising him with different dishes. So far, he hadn't convinced her to move in with him.

He'd known she still needed the little bit of freedom and independence that came with having her own space, and he loved her enough to understand the need and give it to her. Just as long as he had this: her occasional surprise visits that often lasted for days.

They would be getting married; they just hadn't set a date yet. Understandably, she didn't relish a large wedding and promised to let him know when she was ready. Hell, he was ready but refused to rush her.

He walked into his kitchen and the woman he loved with all his heart was bending over to check something in the oven. His gaze roamed over her backside. She had the most delectable and sexiest behind of any woman he knew. It was perfect. As far as he was concerned, everything about Sloan Elizabeth Donahue was perfect.

"Something smells good."

She jerked her head up. She smiled, closed the oven and raced across the room to jump into his arms. His hands immediately went to that backside he'd just been admiring to support her in place.

She wrapped her arms around his neck and smiled brightly at him. "You're early."

He returned her smile. "No, for you I'm right on time. Always."

Her smile seemed to brighten even more. "Yes, always."

And then he kissed her with all the love in his heart. She was his and he was hers. Both he and his family had been there for her two weeks ago when her father had been one of ten businessmen arrested. She had called to talk to her parents but they tried shifting the blame. Saying that if she'd married Harold when they'd wanted her to, then they would have had the money to pay off their extortionist.

Mercury knew some people were better off not becoming parents, and the Donahues were a prime example of those who shouldn't. But then they would not have created this beautiful woman in his arms. Then where would he be? Still a Bad News Steele with the only direction in his life being to some woman's bedroom.

Now he had a purpose, which was to make Sloan

happy. Hell, he'd even made his mother happy by becoming an engaged man. Eden was just waiting for them to give her word so she could start planning what was supposed to be a small wedding. She claimed all she needed were two weeks, and knowing his mother, he had no reason not to believe her. He'd warned Sloan about how big the Steele family was and not to be surprised if a small wedding became a rather large one.

No matter how hellish his days might have been, it was nice knowing he had this. He had her. He broke off the kiss and smiled when he saw how desire filled her eyes.

"I love you, Mercury."

He leaned in and pressed another kiss on her lips. "I love you, too."

"And I'm ready for Eden to start planning our wedding."

He went momentarily still. "You sure?"

She threw her head back and laughed. "Yes! I've never been so sure of anything in my life. I'm ready to be your wife, move in here with you, proudly wear your ring, one day have your babies, take your name, be your life partner in everything. I want it all."

"And I'm going to make sure you get everything you want."

And then he was kissing her again, knowing their lives together would be filled with plenty of love and happiness.

* * * * *

Read on for a sneak peek of
Gannon's story
Claimed by a Steele
by New York Times *bestselling author*
Brenda Jackson.

Gannon Steele held back a laugh as he watched his brother pull the woman he loved into his arms and gave her a whopper of a kiss. It was hard to believe that his *I-will-never-fall-in-love-again* brother had done just that. Fallen in love again.

"Should we think that maybe you're next?"

Gannon glanced over at his oldest brother, Galen. Their parents, Drew and Eden Steele, had given birth to six sons. For years all six had been known around Phoenix as the "Bad News Steeles." Mainly because of their die-hard bachelor ways. Now all of those previous die-hard bachelors were married...all except for Gannon.

Unlike his five brothers, Gannon had never wanted to stay single forever. He viewed marriage as a part of his future. However, he was in no hurry to claim a wife, and now that Mercury was out of the picture, that meant more women for him to enjoy. He couldn't wait.

"You all should know that I'm next, Galen, since I'm the last of the Phoenix Steeles. But I intend to have the time of my life before that happens, which should be for another ten years or more."

"Ten years?" Galen asked, raising a doubtful brow.

"You heard me. Ten years at least. Now that I am the last single Steele left standing, I plan on enjoying being the number one player."

"Be careful, baby bro. You'll be singing a different tune if the right woman appears in your life, trust me."

Gannon chuckled, not taking anything his brother said seriously. He was the master of his own mind and fate. There was no woman alive who could change that.

"Who would have thought?"

Galen lifted a brow. "Thought what?"

"That you would be sounding like Mom in your old age."

Galen frowned. "Be amused all you want, Gannon. Just don't say that I didn't warn you. Do I need to remind you of what happened to me when Brittany appeared in my life? I was the last person anyone expected to fall in love."

Gannon knew that to be true, but then, all one had to do was look at Brittany, or any of the women his brothers had married, to understand how they'd gotten love-whipped. Not only were the women beautiful, but they were intelligent. However, with his current mindset, Gannon figured that even if a beautiful, intelligent woman walked into his life right now, he wouldn't bite. Although he had discriminating taste, he still preferred changing bed partners, and now with his brothers out of the way, there would be even more bed partners out there. He couldn't see settling down to just one woman anytime soon. He would stick to his ten-year plan.

Deciding to change the subject, he said, "So, Zion is having a baby, uh?"

Galen laughed. "No, Celine is pregnant. Zion is strutting around like a damn peacock, like he's the only one who can make a baby. For him to have been the bachelor to hold out the longest to get hitched, it's totally hilarious that he's now all in."

Gannon laughed as well while staring at Zion and the group of men with their wives, all standing together. For years they'd been pegged as the Bachelors in Demand. Now they were all married and seemed pretty damn happy about it. And none of them had wasted time getting their wives pregnant.

As the reception got going in earnest, Gannon's cell vibrated. He checked and saw the caller was Delphine Ryland. He frowned, wondering where he knew that name and why she was listed in his phone contacts. Was she a past bed partner? Although he tried remembering names, he couldn't always do so. Unlike his brothers in their man-whoring days, he didn't have a special phone just for women. If he preferred not talking to one, he just didn't answer. There was also that "decline call" option he utilized whenever he wasn't in the mood.

"When is your interview with *Simply Irresistible*, Gannon?"

He glanced over at his sister-in-law Nikki, who was married to his brother Jonas. The two had announced last week that they were expecting a baby. Gannon's brother Tyson and his wife, Hunter, had announced the same thing a few weeks ago. Gannon figured that was the reason his mother was beaming with pride. She'd seen another son get married off today, which was five out of six, and by this time next year she would have more grandkids to spoil. Hopefully she would give Mercury time to settle into his marriage before waving baby booties in front of him.

"I believe it's this coming week," he said. In all honesty, with the excitement of the wedding, and all his family coming to town, he'd completely forgotten about the interview he'd agreed to do.

Simply Irresistible, a Denver-based magazine, was owned by Chloe Westmoreland, a woman he and his brothers considered a cousin-in-law. Gannon had felt honored when Chloe contacted him to say the magazine would be doing a series of feature stories on CEOs making a difference within their companies. They wanted him to be one of those they highlighted.

Over forty years ago, Gannon's father, Drew Steele, had taken his small trucking company and turned it into a million-dollar industry with routes all over the United States. When Drew retired a few years ago, Gannon had taken over the company as CEO, and he still enjoyed getting behind the steering wheel of a rig himself to make cross-country deliveries and pickups.

He had no problem doing the interview and hoped the feature would help give more respect to the profession of truckers on the road and their importance to a thriving economy. He figured most people didn't think about how businesses depended on the trucking industry to deliver their products to consumers.

"When I talked to Chloe last month, she mentioned that Delphine Ryland would be doing the interview with you," Nikki was saying.

Delphine Ryland.

At some point Chloe had given him the woman's

name and number, and he'd put the contact in his phone list. "Do you know her?"

"Delphine? Yes, I know her."

Gannon shouldn't have been surprised since he knew of Nikki's and Chloe's past working relationship and current friendship. Before Nikki's marriage to Jonas, she had freelanced as a photographer for *Simply Irresistible* on occasion. It stood to reason that she would also know some of the people who worked for the magazine.

"I just missed a call from Ms. Ryland."

Nikki nodded. "She was probably calling to remind you about the interview. Making sure you didn't forget since she was to arrive in town this weekend."

"No problem. I'll return her call tomorrow."

"Delphine's a nice person and a great journalist. You're going to like her, Gannon."

He decided not to say anything to that because he was a man who liked all women, and he figured his feelings for Delphine Ryland would be no different.

Don't miss what happens next in...
Claimed by a Steele
by Brenda Jackson, part of her
Forged of Steele series!

Available May 2020 wherever
Harlequin® Desire books and ebooks are sold.

www.Harlequin.com

Copyright © 2020 by Brenda Streater Jackson

WE HOPE YOU ENJOYED
THIS BOOK FROM

⊕HARLEQUIN
DESIRE

*Luxury, scandal, desire—welcome to
the lives of the American elite.*

Be transported to the worlds of oil barons, family dynasties,
moguls and celebrities. Get ready for juicy plot twists,
delicious sensuality and intriguing scandal.

6 NEW BOOKS AVAILABLE EVERY MONTH!

HDHALO2020

COMING NEXT MONTH FROM

⊕ HARLEQUIN

DESIRE

Available May 5, 2020

#2731 CLAIMED BY A STEELE
Forged of Steele • by Brenda Jackson
When it comes to settling down, playboy CEO Gannon Steele has a ten-year plan. And it doesn't include journalist Delphine Ryland. So why is he inviting her on a cross-country trip? Especially since their red-hot attraction threatens to do away with all his good intentions...

#2732 HER TEXAS RENEGADE
Texas Cattleman's Club: Inheritance • by Joanne Rock
When wealthy widow and business owner Miranda Dupree needs a security expert, there's only one person for the job—her ex, bad boy hacker Kai Maddox. It's all business until passions reignite, but will her old flame burn her a second time?

#2733 RUTHLESS PRIDE
Dynasties: Seven Sins • by Naima Simone
Putting family first, CEO Joshua Lowell abandoned his dreams to save his father's empire. When journalist Sophie Armstrong uncovers a shocking secret, he'll do everything in his power to shield his family from another scandal. But wanting her is a complication he didn't foresee...

#2734 SCANDALOUS REUNION
Lockwood Lightning • by Jules Bennett
Financially blackmailed attorney Maty Taylor must persuade her ex, Sam Hawkins, to sell his beloved distillery to his enemy. His refusal does nothing to quiet the passion between Maty and Sam. When powerful secrets are revealed, can their second chance survive?

#2735 AFTER HOURS SEDUCTION
The Men of Stone River • by Janice Maynard
When billionaire CEO Quinten Stone is injured, he reluctantly accepts live-in help at his remote home from assistant Katie Duncan—who he had a passionate affair with years earlier. Soon he's fighting his desire for the off-limits beauty as secrets from their past resurface...

#2736 SECRETS OF A FAKE FIANCÉE
The Stewart Heirs • by Yahrah St. John
Rejected by the family she wants to know, Morgan Stewart accepts Jared Robinson's proposal to pose as his fiancée to appease his own family. But when their fake engagement uncovers real passion, can Morgan have what she's always wanted, or will a vicious rumor derail everything?

YOU CAN FIND MORE INFORMATION ON UPCOMING HARLEQUIN TITLES, FREE EXCERPTS AND MORE AT HARLEQUIN.COM.

HDCNM0420

SPECIAL EXCERPT FROM

H HARLEQUIN

DESIRE

Putting family first, CEO Joshua Lowell abandoned his dreams to save his father's empire. When journalist Sophie Armstrong uncovers a shocking secret, he'll do everything in his power to shield his family and his pride from another scandal. But wanting her is a complication he didn't foresee...

Read on for a sneak peek at
Ruthless Pride
by USA TODAY *bestselling author Naima Simone*

"Stalking me, Ms. Armstrong?" he drawled, his fingers gripping his water bottle so tight, the plastic squeaked in protest.

He immediately loosened his hold. Damn, he'd learned long ago to never betray any weakness of emotion. People were like sharks scenting bloody chum in the water when they sensed a chink in his armor. But when in this woman's presence, his emotions seemed to leak through like a sieve. The impenetrable shield barricading him that had been forged in the fires of pain, loss and humiliation came away dented and scratched after an encounter with Sophie. And that presented as much of a threat, a danger to him, as her insatiable need to prove that he was a deadbeat father and puppet to a master thief.

"Stalking you?" she scoffed, bending down to swipe her own bottle of water and a towel off the ground. "Need I remind you, it was you who showed up at my job yesterday, not the other way around. So I guess that makes us even in the showing-up-where-we're-not-wanted department."

"Oh, we're not even close to anything that resembles even, Sophie," he said, using her name for the first time aloud. And damn if it didn't taste good on his tongue. If he didn't sound as if he were stroking the two syllables like they were bare, damp flesh.

"I hate to disappoint you and your dreams of narcissistic grandeur, but I've been a member of this gym for years." She swiped her towel over her throat and upper chest. "I've seen you here, but it's not my fault if you've never noticed me."

"That's bull," he snapped. "I would've noticed you."

The words echoed between them, the meaning in them pulsing like a thick, heavy heartbeat in the sudden silence that cocooned them. Her silver eyes flared wide before they flashed with...what? Surprise? Irritation? Desire. A liquid slide of lust prowled through him like a hungry—so goddamn hungry—beast.

HDEXP0420

The air simmered around them. How could no one else see it shimmer in waves from the concrete floor like steam from a sidewalk after a summer storm?

She was the first to break the visual connection, and when she ducked her head to pat her arms down, the loss of her eyes reverberated in his chest like a physical snapping of tautly strung wire. He fisted his fingers at his side, refusing to rub the echo of soreness there.

"Do you want me to pull out my membership card to prove that I'm not some kind of stalker?" She tilted her head to the side. "I'm dedicated to my job, but I refuse to cross the line into creepy…or criminal."

He ground his teeth against the apology that shoved at his throat, but after a moment, he jerked his head down in an abrupt nod. "I'm sorry. I shouldn't have jumped to conclusions." And then because he couldn't resist, because it still gnawed at him when he shouldn't have cared what she—a reporter—thought of him or not, he added, "That predilection seems to be in the air."

She narrowed her eyes on him, and a tiny muscle ticked along her delicate but stubborn jaw. Why that sign of temper and forced control fascinated him, he opted not to dwell on. "And what is that supposed to mean?" she asked, the pleasant tone belied by the anger brewing in her eyes like gray storm clouds.

Moments earlier, he'd wondered if fury or desire had heated her gaze.

God help him, because masochistic fool that he'd suddenly become, he craved them both.

He wanted her rage, her passion…wanted both to beat at him, heat his skin, touch him. Make him feel.

Mentally, he scrambled away from that, that need, like it'd reared up and flashed its fangs at him. The other man he'd been—the man who'd lost himself in passion, paint and life captured on film—had drowned in emotion. Willingly. Joyfully. And when it'd been snatched away—when that passion, that life—had been stolen from him by cold, brutal reality, he'd nearly crumbled under the loss, the darkness. Hunger, wanting something so desperately, led only to the pain of eventually losing it.

He'd survived that loss once. Even though it'd been like sawing off his own limbs. He might be an emotional amputee, but dammit, he'd endured. He'd saved his family, their reputation and their business. But he'd managed it by never allowing himself to need again.

And Sophie Armstrong, with her pixie face and warrior spirit, wouldn't undo all that he'd fought and silently screamed to build.

Don't miss what happens next in…
Ruthless Pride by Naima Simone,
the first in the Dynasties: Seven Sins series,
where passion may be the only path to redemption.

Available May 2020 wherever
Harlequin Desire books and ebooks are sold.

Harlequin.com

Copyright © 2020 by Harlequin Books S.A.

HDEXP0420

Get 4 FREE REWARDS!

We'll send you 2 FREE Books plus 2 FREE Mystery Gifts.

Harlequin Desire® books transport you to the world of the American elite with juicy plot twists, delicious sensuality and intriguing scandal.

FREE Value Over $20

YES! Please send me 2 FREE Harlequin Desire novels and my 2 FREE gifts (gifts are worth about $10 retail). After receiving them, if I don't wish to receive any more books, I can return the shipping statement marked "cancel." If I don't cancel, I will receive 6 brand-new novels every month and be billed just $4.55 per book in the U.S. or $5.24 per book in Canada. That's a savings of at least 13% off the cover price! It's quite a bargain! Shipping and handling is just 50¢ per book in the U.S. and $1.25 per book in Canada.* I understand that accepting the 2 free books and gifts places me under no obligation to buy anything. I can always return a shipment and cancel at any time. The free books and gifts are mine to keep no matter what I decide.

225/326 HDN GNND

Name (please print)

Address   Apt. #

City   State/Province   Zip/Postal Code

Mail to the **Reader Service:**
IN U.S.A.: P.O. Box 1341, Buffalo, NY 14240-8531
IN CANADA: P.O. Box 603, Fort Erie, Ontario L2A 5X3

Want to try 2 free books from another series? Call 1-800-873-8635 or visit www.ReaderService.com.

---

*Terms and prices subject to change without notice. Prices do not include sales taxes, which will be charged (if applicable) based on your state or country of residence. Canadian residents will be charged applicable taxes. Offer not valid in Quebec. This offer is limited to one order per household. Books received may not be as shown. Not valid for current subscribers to Harlequin Desire books. All orders subject to approval. Credit or debit balances in a customer's account(s) may be offset by any other outstanding balance owed by or to the customer. Please allow 4 to 6 weeks for delivery. Offer available while quantities last.

Your Privacy—The Reader Service is committed to protecting your privacy. Our Privacy Policy is available online at www.ReaderService.com or upon request from the Reader Service. We make a portion of our mailing list available to reputable third parties that offer products we believe may interest you. If you prefer that we not exchange your name with third parties, or if you wish to clarify or modify your communication preferences, please visit us at www.ReaderService.com/consumerschoice or write to us at Reader Service Preference Service, P.O. Box 9062, Buffalo, NY 14240-9062. Include your complete name and address.

HD20R